30 Stories About

LIFE & DEATH

HENRI COLT

rake press

30 Stories About

LIFE & DEATH

Copyright © Henri Colt 2022

Printed in the United States of America

The stories herein are works of fiction. All events and characters portrayed are fictitious creations of the author's imagination. Any resemblance to real people or events is coincidental.

All rights reserved. No part of this book may be reproduced in any form or by any electronic or mechanical means, including information storage and retrieval systems, without permission in writing from the publisher, except by reviewers, who may quote brief passages in a review. For information regarding permissions, write to henricolt@gmail.com

ISBN 978-0-9848347-6-1
CIP data available

Printed in the United States of America
Library of Congress
Cataloging-in-Publication Data
Colt, Henri 1956-
Life & Death/Henri Colt
p. cm.
1. Flash Fiction. 2. Short stories
3. Travel. 4. Romance. 5. Erotica. I: Title

Cover design by Richa Bargotra

Grateful acknowledgement is made for permissions to reprint previously published copyrighted stories from: Active Muse, Adelaide Literary Magazine, CaféLit, CommuterLit.com, Cabinet of Heed Magazine, Down in the Dirt Magazine, Fiction on the Web, Flash fiction Magazine, Fewer than 500, Hektoen International Magazine, Holiday Digest, Potato Soup Journal, Red Fez, Scarlet Leaf Review Strands, and Rock and Ice Magazine

Back cover photo by Michele Swift

Published by rake press
Laguna Beach, CA

30 Stories About

LIFE & DEATH

HENRI COLT is a physician, certified philosophical practitioner and international speaker who has lived, worked, and lectured on six continents. In addition to his scientific papers and textbooks, he is the author/editor of the popular *The Picture of Health: Medical Ethics and the Movies* and nonfiction works such as *Modigliani: Art & Illness.* Colt is a medical ethicist and University of California Emeritus Professor of Pulmonary and Critical Care Medicine. When he is not conducting training seminars, dancing tango or climbing mountains, he works on screenplays from his home in Laguna Beach, CA.

§

Life & Death is the first anthology of Colt's previously published flash fiction.

Prologue

I spent my entire career working hard to save the lives. . . of dying patients.

What the hell? A whole lifetime of work, awards, accomplishments where I was able to extend the quality of life for my patients (though at the height of my career I treated extreme cases – those who were terminal by the time they saw me).

And so the very contradiction of life-saving, of a terminal patient, is apparent.

And the relationship I had to Life & Death became a part of me, ultimately finding its way out and onto the page in bursts of visual, beautiful, hard, sad prose. As I traveled the world, both as a lecturer and mountain climber, my travels became the backdrop of my stories.

This little book promises to take you gently by the hand - and sometimes not so gently, sometimes grabbing you and thrusting you - into a moment that is so close to both the thrill of life and the quiet of death.

This little book, if it matters at all, is my attempt to connect to you. Because in both Life & Death, we are always looking to connect to someone.

Henri

Table of Contents

Prologue v

LIFE 1

- Tango 3
- Forever Always 9
- Does Anyone Sing at Easter 14
- In Aristotle's Footsteps 19
- Sticky Lips and The Stray Cat 24
- Breakfast in Tokyo 27
- Something about Chanel 31
- A Girl Named Ahh 35
- Gingerbread Love 41
- My Guardian Angel 44
- The Deer Trail 47
- My Sixtieth Birthday 54
- Alone 59
- Serengeti 101 62
- Eve's Night Out 67

DEATH 71

- Unanswered Questions 73
- Kate Can't Fly 76
- A Cold Little Secret 78
- Too Late for a Kiss 83
- Whisper Red 85
- Kansas City Ganges 90
- Jungbu's Mother 96
- Never a Coward 102
- Sarah's Lesson 108
- A Death in Quito 115
- The Colonel's Daughter 120
- Six Months and Counting 127
- Going South 134
- Qualis artifex pereo 140
- Moroccan Blue 145
- Permissions Acknowledgments 151

LIFE

It was as if the sculptor had discovered the essence of creativity, that moment when suffering ends, and joy spills forth like the birth of an idea.

Tango

"I don't dance the tango," Kyra says, "but I took lessons before coming." She bites into a bright green apple with an audible crunch. Its tangy taste has a whisper of sweetness that disappears on the back of her tongue. Swallowing hard, she looks out from where she is sitting to the Obelisco, an iconic national monument standing like an arrow at the corner of Corrientes and Callas 9 de Julio in downtown Buenos Aires. She dares not say she disliked the robotic T.A.N.G.O ballroom steps she learned back home in Colorado.

"Tango is everything," says Mateo with a shrug. His thick Spanish accent reminds Kyra of Iñigo Montoya in *The Princess Bride*.

She moistens her lips before answering. "I love the music, even if I don't understand the words."

"Most lyrics are Lunfardo, a street-slang spoken by criminals and working-class people." Mateo puts his guampa on the counter. The calabash gourde with its bambilla, a steel straw, is what Argentines traditionally use to drink that caffeine-rich mixture of hot water and dry coca-like leaves called maté.

"Alexa," he commands, walking toward the voice-controlled speakers in the living room. "Play tango."

A suite of mournful melodies shrouds the loft in melancholy. Kyra confidently tugs at her tight black jeans and notices the way her sleeveless tee-shirt accentuates her curves. Perched on the high—backed stool in Mateo's open kitchen, she playfully dangles a black stiletto on her toes. After joyful days sharing lunches and museum visits, this is her first time in his loft apartment. She wonders why he hasn't kissed her yet.

"In tango," he says after a while, "the man leads the woman to where she wants to go."

"Where I want to go?" Kyra smiles. "I thought you guys were macho."

"Well, tango is a conversation." Mateo puts his hand over his heart and feigns a dance step before sitting next to her. "The man leads, and the woman follows, but where he goes depends on where you take him."

"Sounds a lot like good sex." Kyra feels her cheeks flush. She never makes the first move, but watching the way Mateo sipped his maté inspired her.

"It is better than sex," he says calmly. "Tango is love in three minutes, reciprocal and dramatic."

"If tango is better than sex, babe, you haven't been with the right girl." She knows she is falling for him. He is aloof but romantic, secretive, but enchanting like a forbidden fruit.

At the milonga," he chides, "you dance with your partner, but also with others."

She feigns a pout. "I don't think I would like the idea of you holding other women if you were my partner."

He chuckles and loosens his necktie. She admires him from over the lip of a glass of chardonnay. With jet-black hair, a seven-day stubble, and suntanned skin, he could be a Columbian drug lord, but he is a journalist. The truth is, she longs to run her fingers over his wrinkled shirt. She drops her shoe.

"Oops."

Mateo slides from his stool and kneels at her feet. His hands are softer than she imagined, and within moments, she is back in her heels.

"Eu-phoria?" His eyes linger on the small cursive letters tattooed above her ankle.

"It means happiness." Kyra tosses her wavy black hair, exaggerating the sparkle in her eyes. When she stands, her forehead reaches his aquiline nose.

"Teach me to dance the tango," she says.

Mateo puts his right hand firmly on the small of her back, pulling her toward him. She naturally lays her left hand on his biceps. Pressure from his fingers makes her lean into him. She trembles as the back of his free hand slides from her cheek to her shoulders and down her right arm. He squeezes her palm.

"First lesson," he says.

She knows he is a good dancer. They met at Confitería Ideal, a decrepit yet grandiose haunt built in the style of a Parisian salon from the Belle Epoque, with cast-iron balustrades, marble colonnades, and baroque glass chandeliers hanging from high ceilings. Timeless and eternal, it is a place where porteños, those inhabitants of Buenos Aires proper, gather for clandestine encounters and love affairs, a place where friendships and romance are indulged in the space of twelve minutes, the time of a tanda, three songs danced with the same partner. She went there for coffee a few days ago, to people watch and study tango.

Mateo interrupts her thoughts. "We dance milonguero style."

She bites her lower lip. Milongueros take small steps while in a tight embrace, with lots of turns and pivots called giros, created for couples navigating around a crowded dance floor.

"I think that's pretty different from the ballroom steps I learned before," she says.

Mateo's eyes close as if he were talking with her telepathically. A persistent pressure of his hand near her spine shifts her weight onto her toes and lifts her heels from the hardwood floor. Her breasts, hips, and thighs tilt forward until her torso touches his, making a human Obelisco.

Captured in his right arm, without even room to look down, she feels their upper bodies expand and retract together like the bellows of an accordion. A slight hitch of his right shoulder coaxes her hand from his biceps. She rests her forearm on the nape of his neck. It is a moment without past or future, exciting as when lovers discover each other for the first time.

She looks up expectantly. "Like this?"

"Yes."

She can sense the slightest twitch of his body. His deepening breath is a signal to begin, a sign she is safe and secure in his arms.

"Don't think, Kyra" he counsels. "Just be."

When he steps back onto his right foot, she follows, entering the space his open hips make for her. Another step and she feels herself pivoting into a lean with her left foot forward as her right foot gracefully comes to rest off the ground against the back of her left ankle.

"Pause," he whispers, as if the word has two syllables. He rocks her tenderly. Their hands are mere embellishments. "We have time, don't hurry."

She feels his unwavering strength in spite of her exaggerated list. The way his arm envelopes her ribcage in a tight embrace, she feels protected, yet free, clearly taken, but willfully giving.

"Tango is love without noise," he says. "It is life without confusion."

The music's solemn rhythm wraps itself around her heart. Mateo's cheek brushes hers when he dabs the faintest of kisses on her ear. She can almost smell the testosterone. An invisible cloud of warm air escapes his nostrils and floats across her neck, fading into a delicious chill on her shoulders.

Kyra shudders with excitement. Her eyes close. If he moves back any further, I'm going to fall on my face, she thinks, but she isn't frightened. Did she invite him to hold her this way, or did he initiate the lean?

Like a force field springing from her partner's chest, an invisible surge of energy prompts a long step backward onto her right foot. She feels the move before it begins.

She steps. He follows. Their breaths wrestle as lovers do before a long and painful separation. Kyra hears the staccato lament of piano, violin, and that small accordion-like instrument called a bandoneón. 'Tengo miedo de quererte,' sings a porteño with characteristic whiskey and cigarette-filled gruffness. Mateo continues the song in English, his accent heavier than usual:

"I am afraid to love you," he says, "to have you and to lose you, to then feel in me a death when you pass by."

Forever Always

Imre was the illegitimate son of a destitute Hungarian priest, presumably descended from King Stephen and Giselle of Bavaria. I was the son of an Orthodox Jew who escaped to a secular life in Paris. We met in high school, or rather, at the music store next to the school, where my heart fluttered while we played guitars instead of doing math.

Discovering our musical talents, we hustled microphones from a street artist and traded money for an amplifier. Imre's knack for melody and the emotional expression of his falsetto made my lyrics, secretly written solely for him, surreal.

After graduation, we rented a flat near the river. Our reputations grew, as did our success with women. My curly black hair and eye shadow sparked a bad boy image that rivaled my friend's angelic blond and blue-eyed disposition. They treated us like community property, and we played along.

"Maybe you and I should have sex," I said one evening, gathering my courage and pouring Imre another whisky after the girls left. We weren't drunk yet, I thought, so we couldn't deny personal responsibility.

He looked up from the couch. "I thought you would never ask." His outstretched hands beckoned me to sit.

I emptied my glass with a gulp. Whatever hormonally-induced surge of desire makes coupling inevitable suddenly vanished. "You mean, like now?"

He looked surprised. "Why not? But, I need to tell you, I think homosexuality is hereditary."

The alcohol's smoky sweetness lingered on my tongue. "Sexuality is fluid," I stammered, "and ever-changing."

Imre stared at my crotch. "Performance anxiety?" He laughed and reached for his guitar. "Don't worry...."

I pulled mine from behind a chair and joined him in a complex set of chord progressions, wondering why I felt relieved and disappointed at the same time.

We drifted apart after that. I moved out and found work writing articles about musicians. Imre traveled abroad and became a virtuoso. The years passed. When I heard he lived in a famous art-deco building on the outskirts of town, I looked him up, thinking there might be a story.

"Hey," he said after opening the door. He patted me on the back, and I shivered as if we had never parted.

"Do you still play?" he asked, nodding toward a cluster of acoustic guitars on either side of a baby grand piano. The apartment had high ceilings and a library filled with ceramics. Opulent 1920s furniture with muted colors and shiny metal accents squatted every room. He offered me a glass of chardonnay.

I sat on the couch and tried to sip my wine. "Not much," I said. "I mostly write for magazines."

"Huh," he said. "Sounds boring."

I watched him gather his golden hair into a ponytail. His eyes were like the sky, and there was a tenderness there that I suddenly remembered. *Kiss him,* I thought. "It pays the rent," I said instead, "and I'm writing a novel."

He crossed his hands behind his neck. "I live with a guy," he said. "We're lovers."

"My girlfriend is pregnant," I said, "but I wouldn't call her my lover."

He plopped into an armchair. "We're cool about it. He's older than me, and he bought this apartment, so maybe it's serious."

"I'm happy for you." I wondered if he sensed my resentment.

We filled the time talking literature and music. I trashed my idea of an interview, and I couldn't help thinking about what might have been. "I need to catch the train back to the city," I said.

He walked me to the door. "Stay in touch," he said, then hugged me with that one arm hug guys use sometimes. We shook hands too, as if we knew it would be a while before we would see each other again.

And that's how it was.

Twenty-five years later, I saw him on television. Having separated from my second wife, I was in Budapest, researching the Vatican's influence on Sebastian Bach.

Someone told me Imre lived in Eger, a medieval town founded by King Stephen only ninety minutes to the east. I found the number and made a call. We agreed to meet after breakfast.

I drove the scenic route through the Bukk mountains, a heavily forested region of the inner Carpathians, and parked my car at Eger's train station. Narrow, cobblestoned streets lined with bookstores and gaudy souvenir shops led to the Basilica of Saint John the Apostle, guarded by six massive Corinthian columns. Flanked by statues of Saint Peter and Saint Paul, Imre stood at the top of a long flight of stairs.

"You've returned to your roots," I said, breathless. I greeted my friend with a hug.

He smiled. "My 11th-century namesake, Emeric, was killed in a hunting accident in Romania, but he was buried in a town not far from here, in Székesfehérvár."

"How do you pronounce that?"

"Szé-kes-fe-hér-vár. Don't try to spell it."

He beckoned me past an ornate, cast-iron door leading into the church. I was surprised when he crossed himself with holy water from the stoup.

"The frescoes are beautiful," he said.

I looked up at three lavishly decorated cupolas high overhead. Behind me, a pipe organ loomed from the balcony. A painting of the Archangel Michael spearing Lucifer towered over an altar made from white Carrera marble.

"It's been a long time," I said after a minute. I put my hand on Imre's shoulder.

"Too long." He patted my hand and breathed deeply. "You know, after I became famous, I left my lover, got married, and had three kids. Now I'm having an affair with someone twenty years younger than me. How's that for a fuckin' life's work?"

I suddenly felt as if we were back in our small apartment together. "Do you love her?"

"You're assuming a 'she.' Well, it's just a final spurt of testosterone, not a fatal wound from Cupid's arrow. But, to answer your question...no."

The decades melted. *Oh, God.*

"Anyway, I'm a musician, right?" I heard him sigh as he crossed himself before the altar.

"Imre?" I squinted through my suddenly wet eyes, whispering now, "Imre...I loved you."

We stood in silence. "I know," he said, finally. I loved you too. Always."

Does Anyone Sing at Easter

Some stared and marveled at the man's audacity. Others murmured amongst themselves but said nothing to the museum guard, who seemed to have turned a blind eye to what was happening. Deep in the far corner of the room, opposite the open hall that led to a collection of Impressionists' paintings, an older man, in ancient times he would have been mistaken for a sorcerer, stood unmoved by the gathering crowd. His long hair was grey. His mustache flowed over the folds at the corners of his lips, dangling silver, like mercury, it stopped suddenly at the margins where his chin melted into his jawbone as if frozen at the edge of space.

He never removed his eyes from the firm, undulated marble buttock hidden beneath the palm of his right hand. The woman had kneeled at Christ's feet, embracing him, pleading. Her head rested against his belly as if she were worshipping, listening perhaps for his fluttering heart, not in a sexual way, nor sensual, but her hips were flexed and the small of her back turned inwards. A thin line led clearly past the sacral triangle at the base of her spine. Her breasts pushed against the Redeemer, but obviously, he could not hold her. His outstretched arms seemed nailed into the stone as only an impression of the cross remained. His legs bent. Immobile, he stood crucified.

The gallery slowly emptied. Like a nonparticipating and willing observer, the man took it all in, and soon it was quiet in the adjacent corridor that led away from the cloistered space where he stood. In front of him, the suffering seemed real. He kept his cupped hand over the firm sloping surface of the woman's body. He followed the curve upward unto her back, then down into the folds between her legs, downward still onto her thighs until he reached the place in the stone where she knelt alone, desperate, where silence drowned a love that would remain unheard through millennia, yet felt by all women who cry for their lovers, their sons, for the vulnerable and victims lost unjustly, pulled from their grasp into the darkness and utter loneliness of death. Amidst a cloud of loss without remorse, the man suddenly understood, and he remembered his friend's passing. Enveloped in their embrace, he listened to their final words that death was not darkness beckoning but a blessing.

Still, he was afraid, and at that particular moment, he had no thoughts of tranquility. Feeling dejected, he gently slid his hand upward along the woman's buttocks again, passing alongside her spine. He pressed his fingers against the stone as if he could massage her tightened muscles, taught through her upper back and into her naked shoulders. Her head was turned, and her face was barely visible, as if the sculptor had hidden her intentionally to avoid the gaze. Christ's head was also turned, drooped, leaning against her shoulder. It was as if the pain of her embrace needed to be without witnesses and left unexamined. As if it needed to be felt rather than perceived, understood rather than explained, and like the froth of a thousand waves shattering over the rocks only to disperse and evaporate in the mist, her pain still signaled an approaching storm.

Violence was in the air. He felt it, so he raised his head.

And the guard said nothing still.

A tall, black, beautiful woman came to stand by the man's side. Her thighs, though dressed in tights, reminded him of the woman kneeling. Her dark oval eyes radiated intelligence and compassion. Her hair seemed chiseled and pockmarked, crudely draping onto her neck and along her cheeks as if it had been rushedly groomed like the Rondanini Pietà, the unfinished sculpture on which Michelangelo worked to the last days of his life.

Her voice was softly inquisitive, childlike, but with undertones of maturity that echoed in the now-empty gallery.

"Can you feel it?" she said.

"Of course." He barely moved his lips. His hand remained on the sculpture.

She touched the stone gingerly. "Was Rodin thinking of Camille when he made it?"

The man looked and caught her eyes. "You mean Camille Claudel? Yes, most probably. This sculpture dates from around 1894. Her abortion was in 92', but they may still have been intimate. In this piece, it is almost as if it were he on the cross. Rodin was torn then; a classic battle between wife and lover, but perhaps she was already showing signs of emotional instability."

The woman stopped smiling. "Why must men always blame the girl?"

"There is more than only moral suffering here," he said.

"You seem almost obsessed," she said.

She sounded playful, and he wondered if she was testing him, to see how far he might lead her in his labored explanations, so he said nothing. Instead, he lowered his eyes and stared at his hand still caressing the smooth marble finish.

"Your hands are very muscular," the woman said.

"Perhaps she was still his lover," he said after a moment. Then he stepped away from the sculpture, close enough to the wall so he could read the fine print on the exhibit label. He thought of his own work. He also thought of how another artist, Niki de Saint Phalle, had crafted the tombstones of her assistants who died of AIDS in the early years of the pandemic. "Christ and the Magdalene," he read out loud. He noticed the woman followed his gaze back to the bodies hewn from the marble block, polished figures entwined in an embrace that contrasted sharply with the unfinished base. It was as if the sculptor had discovered the essence of creativity, that moment when suffering ends, and joy spills forth like the birth of an idea.

He hoped she might accept his invitation for tea.

In Aristotle's Footsteps

Squatting on a cement slab, the old doctor watched sea urchins bristle their spines in clear Aegean waters. His short brown tunic covered shoulders broad as an oxen's chest. He flexed his tanned, muscular forearms and clenched his fists, then rolled his cotton trousers up to his knees and stood studying the horizon.

There is not much time, he thought. The sea, which moments earlier was flat as shimmering glass, had begun to flutter. Small waves exaggerated by the passing of an outboard motorboat slapped against the concrete breakers. After a sudden splash that sent salty droplets onto his cheeks, he saw a school of fish dart between nearby rocks.

This should be a good place, he murmured to no one in particular. He adjusted his kufi and stepped into the water.

He was used to being alone. Every day he had wandered somewhere around Dikili, a coastal town in the district of Izmir, south of Troy, not far from the ancient city of Pergamum to the East. He squinted to focus clearly on the islands of Garip at the edge of the bay and further still on a land the Greeks called Lesbos.

He had come to Turkey from Stageira, near the remnants of the old city-state, perched on the peaks of a craggy peninsula in central Macedonia. They called him Doctor Aristotolia there, not for his medical skills, but for the way he recited, year after year in ancient Greek, French, English, and even Arabic, the teachings of the great philosopher, Aristotle.

A veritable Peripatetic of old traditions, he loved to walk. Each spring, he headed east across Southern Thrace, past the sobering memorials of more than half a million casualties on the Gallipoli peninsula and across the Dardanelles, the former Hellespont, to Asia Minor. Beyond Çanakkale, he traveled toward the ruins of Assos, where Aristotle had married young Pythias, the adopted daughter of King Hermias. For three months and almost 1000 kilometers, he lived mostly on bread and canned sardines.

Far from living in isolation that would have betrayed the twenty-three-centuries-old teachings of his tutor, he stopped along the way to meet friends and make new acquaintances. He sat in waterfront cafés to indulge in the occasional bottle of Ouzo and Raki, licorice-tasting drinks he could afford thanks to coins thrown to him by generous tourists. He played cards with the fishermen and backgammon with the school children, ministering also to their rashes and sniffles. "Every object in the universe has a purpose for which it exists," he told them, "and you are no different."

Townspeople gathered around him to take counsel about what was good, true, and how to live a conscious life. "Do not fear taking responsibility for your happiness," he said, "and live well. To learn and wonder about the world using all of our senses makes us human, for the good is simple. But tardy not to become true to yourself," he would say, "for we are in a race against time."

Arriving in Assos, known under the modern name of Behramkale, he always climbed the rocky promontory to the ancient Temple of Athena. This year, he had stayed only three days. Comfortably seated beneath its Doric columns, he gathered his thoughts, to divorce them from those engrained on his heart by the great philosopher. Like Aristotle, his physician-father taught him much, and he was orphaned when barely a teenager. He obtained scholarships to the best universities and was schooled first in Athens, then Paris and Oxford in both philosophy and mathematics, but later abandoned an academic career to travel the world and write. At fifty, he was in Lesbos, and two years later married and settled in Stageira, Aristotle's birthplace.

Like every year for twenty years, he would leave Assos and continue his way along the rugged coast to Dikili, near the plain of Atarneus. It was here, long ago, that his wife had died with his unborn child, the result of his mishandling an uncommon complication of her pregnancy. She was very young, much younger than he, and bright, and kind, and talented in the languages of love. She cared nothing for material things but shared with him all she thought was sacred and joyous. Her loss had pained him and pained him still.

Now, the doctors had told him they had little to offer him, and the abdominal cramps would soon return. So today, for one moment only, he would ask to be forgiven for the tragedy of having lost the ones he loved. Like for the ancient Greeks, the ritual of his sacrifice would appease the gods. It would remind him that unlike trees and animals, each of our decisions can be a rational choice, but that overwhelmed with emotions we can be unreasonable and that our mistakes, however terrible, also make us human.

He was already a decade older than was Aristotle when he died, and this could be his final act rather than travel to Chalkis, across the sea on the Greek island of Euboea. It was the place where Faistida, Aristotle's mother was born, and where coincidently, his own mother, Celestine, had raised him in a small cottage with a garden surrounded by olive trees.

The man sensed rather than saw what hid beneath the slime-covered rocks next to his feet. He plunged his hands into the water, and when they emerged from the bay with a listless white and maroon octopus, his tunic and trousers were quite wet. He scrambled over jagged rocks, clinging to the animal as it labored for its life. The reflection of his embroidered kufi glittered momentarily from the sun on the water's surface. Grappling his way across an iron-clad pontoon, he jumped onto a wooden dock the size of a small dining table. He then saw that the animal's struggle had been in vain.

He shuddered as if the death-spiral he had witnessed had been his own. Picking up the now lifeless creature, he said a silent prayer, not to God, but to Nature and the Cosmos for the cyclical changes Aristotle once called a continuous coming-to-be that made life as near to eternal as possible. After stepping onto the beach, he pushed the octopus's head through its mouth, turning it inside out. Then he cleaned it by removing the ink pouch before rubbing out its eyes, and he threw the innards to the fish. Seagulls overhead squawked with excitement, their forward-slanted wings signaling an aerial attack. He solemnly buried what was left of the octopus and moved on.

A young woman with a dark complexion, wearing blue jeans, a light tunic, and a hijab, was seated on a small ledge above him. She was possibly a refugee, he thought, and she was crying. He imagined how watching him might have raised untold emotions. He stopped rather than pass her by.

"As-salamu-alayka," he said. "May peace be upon you."

She seemed surprised he had addressed her in Arabic.

"Wa alaikum assalam wa rahmatu Allah," she stammered according to Muslim custom. "And to you be peace together with Allah's mercy." She acknowledged his greeting with one of greater respect and kindness.

He requested permission to sit beside her on the ledge. Tears continued to fall softly from her pale green eyes, but he waited. When she finally spoke and told him her story, he listened patiently, for there are times when the greatest philosophers know to remain silent.

Sticky Lips and The Stray Cat

My girlfriend and I had just returned from an overnight trip into Manhattan. A night of gentle love-making on the pillow-covered king size bed at The Surrey followed drinks at the Carlisle and dinner on seventy-sixth and Madison. Our morning walk across Central Park in a light summer rain kept us in a tender mood, but the drive back to Westchester was mostly silent, each of us locked in our own thoughts. After getting out of the car, I escorted Chris to the front door.

"I can't stay, you know."

"Awww," she said. "Baby is so important he just has to get back to the office."

I put my hand on her waist. "It pays the bills," I said. Then jokingly, "I didn't see you change this morning. Are you still wearing a little bit of nothing under your dress?"

She turned and bent slightly forward to slip her key into the front door. "Just nature's natural fur," she said without looking up.

I nudged her from behind, putting my hand on the back of her short, knit skirt. I could almost feel the warm, soft triangle between her legs. My palm cupped her snuggly. Nestling her, I wrapped my arm around her waist. Her thighs squeezed me…hard.

She leaned her cheek on my shoulder. "Hmmm," she said, pressing herself against me. I kissed her behind the ear and inched my lips down toward the tip of her nose. I scratched the nape of her neck playfully.

"Stop," she whispered, "you know I like that."

"You could undress here, you know?

She giggled, but it sounded more like a purr. "You mean on my doorstep? I don't think so. I have neighbors."

"They'll just be jealous."

"They'll gossip."

"Let them talk." I brushed myself against her. The word 'relentless' popped into my mind.

"I'm serious," she said. "Stop."

But my hand was still trapped between her legs. I sort of just left it there, fiddling, as if it had a mind of its own.

"Stop," she said, in a way that made the word sound like it had two syllables. I restrained a smile when I felt the tautness in her thighs relax. Grudgingly, but with my arm still wrapped around her waist, I grasped her hand and lifted it to my lips. A sweet almond aroma rose from my fingertips. I breathed deeply, making sure she would hear me.

"Did I upset you?" she said.

"I'm not sure," I ventured. "Maybe it's the mixed messages?"

"It's just a word," she said. "There's no need to make a big thing about it." Pulling away, she adjusted her skirt and turned the key. The door popped open and she stepped across the threshold, then pivoted on her toes. I loved her toes, but they were concealed in those soft black loafers she bought on Lexington Avenue. No socks.

With her back to the hallway, she looked at me. I marveled at the way she ran her tongue across her teeth and scratched the corner of her mouth with her little finger, as if she were removing a spot of lipstick.

"My lips get so sticky," she said, suddenly opening the cross-body Hermes bag draped over her shoulder. She pulled a tube of lipstick from the purse. Its black and gold logo was unmistakable. With perfectly set short black hair, a shapely figure, and deep blue eyes, she stood statuesque-like in the doorway. I peeked past her at the small marble coffee table covered with books. A crystal vase overflowed with bright yellow tulips. The lights came on automatically.

"I had a wonderful time," she said, "but you know that."

I wasn't sure whether to leave or to wait patiently for an invitation to come in. Perhaps she expected me to say goodbye. A stray cat sauntered across the driveway and brushed against my leg, arching its back repeatedly. After curling itself twice around my ankles, it groaned plaintively before vanishing into the shadows of an afternoon sun drowning in the treetops.

Breakfast in Tokyo

Love is like food. Take it away, and feel the hunger. Lose it, and life is a starving nightmare. My therapist says I have abandonment issues because I miss the symbiosis of my mother's womb, but it's as natural to need love as it is to eat, and I've wanted food since I was born.

It's a ninety-minute ride to downtown Tokyo. I stare out the window and marvel at how silently the bullet train glides past row upon row of wooden homes. Their gabled roofs of slate tile remind me of how I stack tablets of dark chocolate on my kitchen counter. The man beside me is garrulous in his complaints about his wife. The smell on his breath betrays a preference for scotch over bottled water, so I chomp on wasabi beef chips and chug a soda to drown his words.

When the doors slide open, I lunge onto the platform of Shinjuku Station, a bustling artery of shops and eateries bursting with the overwhelming smells of udon noodles and teriyaki. People converge there twenty-four hours a day, seven days a week. I am jostled like seaweed in a tidal surge. An old man with a briefcase is glued to my side, trapping me in a human wave moving toward the exit, and I feel as powerless as the day my mother left me.

I tower over hundreds of dark suits rushing by like a school of sardines returning to their feeding grounds. A teenage girl giggles conspicuously, covering her mouth with tiny hands. My stomach tightens with the feeling that she is mocking me. Like my life, the broken wheel on my suitcase is a nuisance. I clatter by a pink bouquet of hearts painted on a windowpane, signaling the entrance to a love hotel whose temptations I ignore.

As I exit the terminal, a woman wearing shiny gold Gucci sneakers and a trendy business suit cups her ears. She is visibly annoyed by the rattle of my carry-on. I flick my hand to dismiss her, but immediately regret the rudeness of my action. After hustling across the avenue, I drag my bags up the granite steps to my hotel. It has all the amenities of luxury real estate, like toilets with heated seats, a minibar, and bowls of fruit in every room.

"Konbanwa." The girl at the registration desk sings the greeting and bows her head.

I try to smile. "Good evening," I say. I am so close to the wall that I can touch the gray-linen curtains dressing the hotel's floor-to-ceiling windows. A young woman who looks like a Sakura princess in tights and running shoes walks past. She stops three feet from where I stand and gazes toward the lobby. Her long silver hair flows to the small of her back. It swishes when she puts a cell phone to her ear.

The receptionist interrupts my cinematic voyeurism. "May I have your passport, please?" Her outstretched palms reach across the counter.

I hand over my papers and watch her impeccably manicured nude fingernails slide over the keyboard. I survey the lobby, but my princess in tights is gone.

Damn, she was beautiful.

I go to my suite on the 38th floor and devour a bowl of strawberries. By the time they are gone, all I can think about is her—my princess.

The suddenness of falling in love comes on like hunger pangs. My mind explodes into a new dimension—a way of being that isn't of this world. I sit in front of the minibar and go to war with a bag of pretzels. I guzzle cognac and imagine things, maybe the girl's slender fingers curled around her chopsticks. They say we all have a soul mate somewhere. Perhaps she's the one; my unicorn, the Penelope to my Ulysses, my Helen without Troy.

I go to bed overwhelmed with joy, but my sleep is restless. In the morning, the growl of my empty stomach signals a bitterness caused by prophetic visions of abandonment.

Downstairs, I avoid the lavish breakfast buffet and order eggs from the menu. I pour myself some tea.

A cell phone chimes. The 'Hello Kitty' logos glued to a jeweled iPhone set on a nearby table smother my field of view. I recognize the owner immediately. *She's younger than me, maybe twenty.* It's hard to tell a Japanese woman's age.

Her face is slim, with high cheekbones and a small rounded nose. Her baby-blue eyeshadow accentuates her monolid almond eyes. There is blush on her cheeks, pale pastels like cherry blossoms in early spring, and her lips barely move when she smiles.

She answers her phone.

A high-tied ponytail of razor-straight silver hair falls onto the pink tweed jacket covering her blouse. I take a deep breath and clumsily pound a hardboiled egg with my chopsticks.

Princess has elegant fingers—she wears no ring. Before I can walk over to introduce myself, she swipes up and drops the phone into her clutch. I catch her gaze, but she lowers her chin and stares at her breakfast plate.

She slides the tip of her knife under a slice of tomato that she lays over the soft yellow yolk of a fried egg. She cuts away the whites with surgical precision, then scoops a tiny mound of rice into a porcelain soup spoon. She slips the spoon beneath the yolk and coaxes it to her lips. She raises her eyes.

When she sees me, I panic. *Please, don't go*, I want to shout. *I'm not some crazy stalker*. As she jumps from her seat, I catch a glimpse of ivory skin high beneath the miniskirt that covers her boyish hips. She prances past without a glance, and the sweet vanilla bouquet of Japanese rose, *Kerria japonica*, lingers for a moment, then vanishes in her wake.

Something about Chanel

"It's just sex," she said.

Kelley slipped on her stockings as I watched, her body still covered with sweat from our recent love-making. I was lying on the floor, naked except for my socks.

"It's never just sex," I said. I looked at the messy pile of clothes at her feet, hoping she might toss me a shirt. Instead, she continued to dress hurriedly. I had obviously overstepped her boundaries.

"Don't 'hmph' me again from behind that cute smile of yours," she said. "Anyway, I told you, I'm not falling in love with you."

I playfully cocked my head and puckered my lips.

She laughed. "Don't do that."

"I don't get it," I said. "I presumed we were exclusive. You said that you didn't sleep with someone for the hell of it, and you haven't had sex since what's his name, so I figured if you slept with me, it was special." The music from my stereo grew louder. "Besides, we've known each other for months."

"I don't need to love you to have sex," she said.

"No need to raise your voice, Kelley. Look, I'm sorry if it sounds like I'm making demands, but I thought we were more serious, you know?" I wondered if I had misread her signals. Or maybe she missed something.

Kelley's squint was barely perceptible. "Why?" she said. "Because I finally had you inside me? It's fun, okay? You make me happy."

I restrained a smile. "We're in the fashion industry. Happy is our business."

She stood over me in her printed lace stockings. "And you work for me, right? So don't be stupid," She put her hands on her hips. "And don't be so untrusting."

"I'm not untrusting." Considering I had just complained about her going out every evening, that didn't sound smart. "I can only see you alone on weekends," I said. "What am I supposed to think?"

"You're supposed to think that our dating doesn't give you the right to reign over me," she declared. "Besides, "I've been around." Turning her back to me, she stepped across the room, grabbed the remote control, and hit the mute button. Silence replaced the notes of a Mozart sonata. I sat cross-legged and numbly reached across the floor for my underwear. I wondered why she never had the bunion on her right foot removed.

Kelley rolled her eyes and shrugged. "You even had the gall to say you would teach me to love again, remember?"

I got up and pulled my briefs on the old-fashioned way, one leg at a time. It was a bit comical, but sliding into them with my butt on the floor didn't feel right.

"That's not quite accurate," I said. "You were upset. We were talking about what's-his-name."

"Jason." She spat it out.

"You see, you're still angry about what he did." I couldn't tell her that I wanted her to love me, only me.

"You're probably a bigger narcissist than he is," she said. "Why would I need you in the first place?"

I sat at my desk and pulled on my jeans. "Need me or want me," I said. "It's not the same thing." I watched her bend over to position her pendulous breasts judiciously into a double D bra she held in both hands like a sling. She straightened her torso, and everything was in place by the time she fastened the clasp between her shoulder blades. It was like watching a fisherman cast his net over a school of sardines.

"Aren't you going to wash before you leave?" I asked.

She scrambled the papers on my desk to find her car keys. "I don't have time," she said, "and I don't want to."

An uneasy feeling stirred in my gut. I knew Jason had called her again. Somehow, she sensed my flare of insecurity.

"If you're going to ask if I'll be unfaithful, the answer is I don't know," she said.

"Kelley, look, I never meant for..."

Then she pushed me, laughing. I watched her pull on her skirt and button her blouse. It was one of those python-print pieces by Roberto Cavalli, all crepe-de-chine silk with a ruffled mock neckline and cascading bib. Its long sleeves hid the subtle flabbiness of her upper arms.

"What are you staring at," she said. "I'm not one of those flat-assed bimbos you put on the runway."

I wanted to get up before answering, but she put her hands on my chest and sat me back down.

"Look," she said, "I'm telling you I'm not going to fall in love with you. I'm not going to call you every five minutes, but that doesn't mean I don't want to be with you. When you want to see me, you have my number, and you know where I live."

She took her hands from my chest and stepped across the room, draping a black Ecuadorian shawl over her shoulders. It was of her own design, and it matched the large leather bag now in her hands. I marveled at how she stood into her shoes and adjusted her hair. Streaks of grey were faintly visible. She leaned into the mirror, pouting as she applied her lipstick. Everything about her made me want her again. I was about to stand when she turned and walked toward me with a matter-of-fact look on her face. She knelt and tapped me on the chin, then rose to kiss me with an audible smack that I knew left a glossy red imprint of her lips on my forehead. When she dabbed her teeth with a handkerchief from her bag, I couldn't help but notice the unmistakable fragrance of Chanel no. 5.

"Ciao," she said, and turning on her heels, she left.

A Girl Named Ahh

The only seasons in Bangkok are hot and hotter than hot. When it's hot, the city is covered in smog, not fog from early morning onward. When it's hotter, and the sun finally settles, its bright red glow is buried by an invisible skyline and pollution-filled haze that bodes ill for future generations.

Tourist boat number five was a gaudily painted wooden boat with yellow plastic seats arranged two-by-two in rows. A dozen lifejackets hung like hard orange candy over the pilot's cabin. Along with a horde of photography-addicted Chinese tourists, it took me across the harbor from the Grand Palace to the shopping plaza, past the Riverview and Sheraton hotels, through raw sewage teeming with dead fish and styrofoam.

I left the boat and wandered along crowded back streets filled with little girls in dark green uniforms. Their long black hair was braided. Prancing about in single file, they looked alike and shined like horses on parade. Boys were in uniform too, but acted boisterous and free as if they had just escaped from school. The lapels of their khaki shirts were embroidered with gold medallions bearing semblance to the King.

A swarm of Germans hovered around a crossed-legged Buddha. An old French couple complained about the noise. A teenager wearing a knee-length pleated skirt and white blouse chattered aimlessly, showing her friends the imitation leather clogs on her unstockinged feet. Some older boys with tired smiles watched from a distance. The girl stopped at an ice cream shop with her classmates, laughing.

My guide is late.

A smell of putrid meat drowns my senses. Locals are picking durian and rotten fruit from trash strewn about over nylon tarps.

"Don't people get their food at the Floating Market?" I ask a vendor.

"We no go there," he says. "Market only for tourists. Easier to buy food at 7-Eleven." He points out a few morsels on the table behind him. Carcasses of dried fish in styrofoam platters wrapped in cellophane are scattered across his wooden cart. Just like the shit I saw floating in the harbor.

I kick a pile of discarded cigarette butts into the murky waters of the Chao Phraya. I wonder if God will forgive me.

It's a miracle my guide finds me on the street dead-ending at the river bank. He's from the northern hill regions, with ancestors who fought the Burmese in Ayutthaya, the country's ancient capital eighty miles north of Bangkok.

We walk to a palace with a small temple and a gold-covered reclining Buddha. Its head is propped on the palm of its hand like it's sleeping. I take a minute to walk around.

Guide-man removes his sandals before kneeling at the altar. He lights some incense, then touches his forehead to the concrete floor and murmurs something.

"What did you pray for?" I ask afterward.

"Happiness," he says.

"What the fuck is happiness? I thought Buddhists are supposed to be content with their lot."

"Happiness is to have money," he says.

"Money? Yesterday you said financial rewards are meaningless."

"I have no money myself." He lowers his head. "My wife takes most of all I earn...I give what remains to the temple."

"So, why do you want money?"

"No money, no honey."

"What?"

"Come," he says, "I take you for special massage we call Ab Ob Nuat."

He grabs my arm and huddles me into a pink taxi that weaves in and out of traffic, between heavy machinery and decrepit buildings under construction. After turning into the parking lot of an affluent neighborhood, we stop under a giant sign that has "Paradise" written over it in bold gold letters.

We struggle out from the backseat and climb marble steps toward a spacious lobby. My guide points to a theater-sized lounge inside. "My gift," he says. "For you."

A couple dozen gorgeous young girls are sitting on rows of luxuriously upholstered leather chairs set on a well-lit stage with black and gold curtains. Some paint their faces; others brush their hair. One stares into space and smiles. The most scantily clad are in front with their eyes glued to something in the orchestra pit below them.

"We watch the girls, they watch TV," a muscular, barrel-chested Australian shouts from a nearby table. He grins stupidly and gives me a thumbs-up sign.

A woman wearing a pantsuit and cream-colored blouse strides across the lounge to greet us. She shakes my hand, then whispers something to my guide. Her teeth are ivory. The fine pencil line around her eyelids exaggerates the natural slant of her engagingly dark eyes. With two raised fingers, she signals a waitress for a couple beers and a bottle of Chivas. Magically, my glass is filled to the rim—not a drop of foam overflows.

The woman must be Chinese. She's tall, so I presume she's from the North. Maybe she's the owner. She pulls a notepad from her Chanel purse and jots something on its gold-embossed pages. My guide points to a girl sitting at the back of the stage. The owner nods approvingly. They laugh like they're old acquaintances.

The girl on stage moves to an empty chair in the first row. She's wearing a see-through designer shirt and a miniskirt that couldn't be shorter and still be called a skirt. She crosses her ankles in that way girls do to tease men with glimpses of the soft skin of their upper thighs.

Her ebony hair is in a long, blunt-cut ponytail that reaches the small of her back. Her slender legs dangle like endless promises, surprising for an Asian woman of small stature. Her fingernails are manicured, but unpainted, and if she has lipstick, it must be light. Her breasts seem real because they're small, like cupcakes--unless she's a lady-boy.

"She is for you," my guide says.

"What is her name?"

"Her name is Ahh."

"Ahh?"

"Yes."

The girl smiles and steps down from the stage. They say the most beautiful women in Thailand aren't usually women at all, but this is the real thing.

"Very good time," my guide says. "You take bath, but first, we drink." We empty our glasses with one gulp. Three double shots of Chivas quickly follow.

Perched on her four-inch heels, Ahh's slender hips and trifling baby-fat love handles whisper, hold me. When she spins around playfully, I think I'm going to have a heart attack.

"I am Ahh," she says, touching my arm. "What is your name?"

"My name is George," I lie.

"Like George Washington," she says, laughing discreetly through her perfectly-shaped lips. But her smile makes me sad.

What happened next doesn't matter. I drop three hundred dollars on the table, more than enough to pay for the beers, whiskey shots, and a few minutes of the girl's time. Then I leave because when it's hot in Bangkok, it's hotter than hot, and smog obscures a skyline barely visible from the riverboats that cruise brown waters littered with dead fish and styrofoam.

Gingerbread Love

An uncustomary December rain drenched the sidewalk outside the Laguna village bookstore. Leafing through a book held in her open palms, a cluster of bangles jingling on her wrist, a woman about my age, with shapely hips and a slim waistline, lifted her eyes.

"Can I help you?" she said, pausing to brush a lock of grey hair from her forehead. "Are you looking for anything in particular?"

Richard Dana's "Two Years Before the Mast" beckoned me from the bookshelf but was beyond my reach behind her shoulders.

"Have you read it?" she said. "It's a marvelous piece of local history."

"Indeed." I pointed at the book in her hands. "Did you know Dana's son married Longfellow's daughter?"

"That's an interesting bit of trivia." She put "Hiawatha" back in the bookcase. For a moment, the spicy aroma of her perfume filled the shop. "Are you a historian?"

"My wife taught American literature. After she passed away, I retired and moved to Laguna."

"I'm sorry."

There was an awkward silence, the kind you feel after you've said something wrong, and can't think of words to make things right.

"It's been many years," I mumbled, "but grief can be numbing."

"I lost my husband three years ago, I understand."

It's funny how, when you're on the verge of sharing more about yourself than you probably should, feelings for another can make you take the "I" out of the equation. I wanted to know more about this woman.

"Letting go is hard," I said. The pearls around her neck glistened beautifully on the tapestry of her cashmere sweater. Rolling them between her fingers, she seemed wistful.

"I'm sorry," I said, "I didn't mean to intrude.

"It's nothing," she said solemnly. "We used to love the holidays in Laguna. My husband was a second-generation Lagunatic. Christmas cookies, apple cider, and watching Santa ride down Forest Avenue were a family Christmas tradition."

"Hospitality night is tomorrow evening, isn't it? I saw the announcement in Stu News. I haven't gone in years..."

"Don't you love it, though? Watching teenagers out on their first date, young couples with strollers, and so many smiles..."

There was an unexpected, albeit fleeting joy in her voice. I realized I didn't know her name, nor did she know mine. "I don't mean to be rude," I said, "I mean, I haven't asked someone out in a very long time." I prayed she hadn't seen the way I had to wipe my hands on the back of my jeans.

She smiled and pulled "Two Years Before the Mast" from the shelf. The drawing on the paperback cover was almost an exact copy of the Pilgrim, just like the replica of Richard Dana's tall ship anchored in the nearby harbor.

"I'd love to join you," she said, handing me the book. "I'll bring you some of my gingerbread cookies, unless you're allergic."

When she laughed, I felt as if my past had somehow become fused with the present, as if the youthful exuberance that entered my soul had brought years of solitude to rest and filled my heart with hope.

My Guardian Angel

Maurice lazes by his sleeping bag on a stretch of sparkling green grass across from the village beach. Dozens of raucous seagulls compete for food with tourists on the boardwalk, but Maurice is not a tourist. He used to live in the village, in a cottage with a real kitchen and a back yard and a barbecue. He lived less than a block from his children's school, and not a mile from the small shop where his wife worked as a salesperson.

That was before the pandemic.

After Jenny died, Maurice sent the kids to stay with his mother in the city. He had become ill himself, and could not muster the strength to care for them and keep his job at the gas station. It was hard enough coming home after work to a house where his wife's smile had kept the family together and him off the bottle. Now, the house was empty. The bourbon had changed to wine, and there was never enough of it.

After he lost his job, he could no longer pay the rent. The landlord said his own financial situation forced him to move back into the home, but he gave Maurice a month to vacate the premises. Maurice went to the bank to ask for a loan, but his credit was poor. He had used all of his savings, and maxed out his cards to pay for Jenny's hospital bills and the six months of rehabilitation he needed after his stroke. He did not die from the virus, but its effect on his immune system plugged up his arteries. He spent four weeks in the intensive care unit before he returned home, still able to walk, but his thinking was not as clear as it used to be.

A lanky, old fellow with long brown hair and a surgical mask flopped down beside him on the lawn. His voice was hoarse, his tone was cantankerous. "God damn fools around here don't wear masks or listen to the Governor," he said, pointing at the crowd of young people gathering by the lifeguard station.

Maurice thought of his own mask folded neatly in his shirt pocket and stared dumbly at the old man. His face, or what he could see of it, was tanned and wrinkled. His hair was streaked with yellow as if it had been bleached by the tropical sun, and his eyes were a grayish-blue with flecks of gold. He must be a surfer, Maurice thought, someone from around here with lots of money.

The old man spoke as if no one was listening. "I usually crash at the shelter," he said, "but the cops won't bother me here, and the view is unbeatable. Most days, I buy food at the market and take the shuttle to surfer's cove. It's free, you know." His raised, bushy eyebrows beckoned a response.

Maurice turned his head the other way. He didn't want to be within six feet of a stranger, especially without his mask.

A policeman rode past on a bicycle. A couple of pelicans hovered over the grass like protecting angels.

Protecting what? Maurice did not want to get sick again, but the way his life was going, if he did, maybe death would be a blessing. He got to his knees and stuffed his sleeping bag into the shopping basket he had swiped from the supermarket.

"Where are you off to so fast? The old man grabbed Maurice by the elbow. "I didn't scare you, did I?"

"Please let go of me, sir." Maurice shrugged his shoulders and pushed the man's hand off his arm.

The old man chuckled. "Everyone has gone berserk since the pandemic," he said. "There ain't no humanity left nowhere."

Maurice started to leave.

The old man's raspy voice was barely audible. "Sit down, why don't you?"

With a glance over his shoulder, Maurice saw the man pull a small watermelon from the plastic cooler he had been carrying. His eyes widened with anticipation.

What they shared next was round, lifelike and swollen, smooth, and plump. The shiny red fruit seemed to glitter like a ruby, and when the old man offered Maurice a piece, it was juicy and firm at first bite, but quickly turned soft and sweet. Its white crust seemed little more than the protective layer of a speckled jade shell. For a man who had lost everything, even its seeds were succulent.

The Deer Trail

"Ezra, get up! It's a beautiful morning, and you're sixteen today!" I playfully shook my son's shoulder.

"It's six o'clock, Dad, what are you doing?" He buried his head under his pillow and slid under the covers.

"We're going hiking, remember?" Every year, rain or shine, we skipped breakfast and hit the trail on his birthday. It did not matter if he was tired, sore from baseball practice, or if it was a school day. It did not matter if my patients complained or if I had to cancel a meeting.

"I already made sandwiches and stashed away some protein bars," I said after jamming my first aid kit and a few water bottles into my backpack. I tossed Ezra's hiking boots at the foot of the bed. "Come on, let's go!"

My wife and I had made a habit of taking the kids rock climbing in the California backcountry when we had the time, but whenever we drove to the mountains, it was the same circus. She would keep her headphones on while my gym-climber daughter insisted on leading because she was better and faster than her brother.

I would turn up the radio and let the teenagers have at it in the back seat. We would usually settle the affair by pairing up and exchanging leads. Birthdays were different, though, and today, it was only my boy and me—no risky business— just a safe hike in the woods behind our cabin.

The trail into the San Jacinto National Forest was a short walk from the road heading out of town. For the next few hours, we pushed up dirt with our boots in silence, climbing close to 1500 feet to Tahquitz and its famous towering rock face that dominated the horizon. I wondered what Ezra was thinking, if he was thinking at all. I watched him lunge one foot mechanically after the other ten steps ahead of me.

"I'll never understand how you can walk that fast and text without stumbling," I said. No answer.

"Ezra?" "What?"

"Have you ever thought about putting your phone away?"

"I was checking the weather." He did not look up or break stride.

"Anything exciting?"

He waited for me to catch up. "They're calling for wind this afternoon," he said. "It's been pretty hot."

"We'll be okay," I said. "We have plenty of water."

"I wasn't worried about the water. Well, anyway, how's your ankle?"

"It couldn't be better." There was no need to tell him the pain started when we hit the trail—three sprains in less than a year. The orthopod wanted me to stay in rehab, but there wasno way I could take time off with my busy hospital schedule.

Ezra stashed his phone and started up the trail again. When I was his age, I would not have been caught dead with my father on a day hike. I would have been celebrating with friendsand talking about girls. My boasts were nothing more than juvenile bluster to hide my insecurity and manage teenage anxiety. Ezra was different. He was not the most intelligent kid in his class,but he was smart, although a bit childish.

His girlfriend, Cleo, was a year younger and still a sophomore. My wife worried they'dhad intercourse, but Ezra always shunned our attempts to talk about sexual responsibility and contraception. I decided to nudge him a little.

"Hey Ezra," I said. "Do you think sperm think?"

He glanced over his shoulder and rolled his eyes. He probably sensed I would asksomething personal sooner or later.

"I don't know, Dad. You're the psychiatrist."

"Some men impregnate women more often than others," I said. "Maybe their sperm aresmarter?"

"Or, maybe they're not." Ezra picked up the pace. He took two long steps for each of mine, sliding up the trail like a cross-country skier. I pulled my hiking poles from my pack andsnapped them open as I walked. I did not want him to get too far away.

"I read that exercise and special diets improve sperm strength and stamina.""Vitamins are good, Dad."

I continued. "What do you think about natural testosterone boosters?" "Huh? I don't think about testosterone."

"Well, you will be someday," I shouted. "When you reach my age."

Ezra stopped in his tracks and waited for me to catch up again. "Dad?" he said.

"What?"

"Sometimes, I don't know which of us is a teenager."

I knocked off his baseball cap and stabbed him in the foot with my walking pole. Then we sat on a burnt-out log and shared a protein bar.

"A thousand years ago, Indian sages described the male performance virtues of a plant called *Mucuna Pruriens* in an Ayurvedic text called *The Charaka Samhita*," I said between bites. "It's also known as velvet bean, and it's used for snake bites. You studied Ayurveda for that report last semester."

"Yep."

"And Chinese men believe rhinoceros horn cures impotence. That is why they are going extinct in Africa."

"Chinese men are going extinct in Africa, Dad? Eh, I don't think so."

"Very funny, Ezra."

"If you're worried, Dad, you can buy Sperm Motility Boost on the Internet. Are you and mom planning another kid?"

I laughed. "Absolutely not, but you do know sperm is an endangered species."

Ezra handed me a bag of peanuts. "Sperm is not a species," he said.

"Details, details. Climate change and receding glaciers threaten our survival, but spermcounts fell from 113 to 66 million per milliliter in fifty years. That's a reproductive crisis in themaking."

He pulled out his water bottle. "What's your point, Dad?"

"My point is that despite dwindling numbers, it only takes one to fertilize an egg andmake a baby."

I thought he was going to choke. When he finished coughing, he said, "You're hilarious.

Is that your way to tell me to be careful?"

"I'm just saying the egg is the origin of all questions. It's the inspiration for Hamlet's 'tobe or not to be.' It's the source of every chicken's predicament."

"Okay, you're nuts."

"No, really." I stood to make a big oval egg sign with my hands for emphasis. Then I popped a handful of peanuts into my mouth. "Sperm attack an egg the way teenagers cram into aMiley Cyrus concert."

Ezra laughed so hard I thought his head would burst. "Jeez, Dad, nobody crams into a Miley Cyrus concert anymore."

With that, he grabbed my arm to pull himself up. I guess I didn't steady myself enough, or perhaps he was heavier than I expected, but I fell forward and tripped over the log. While trying to regain my balance, I twisted my ankle.

"Shit." I immediately knew I could not put weight on it. I hobbled over to my backpack and rummaged for my first aid kit. Ezra looked worried. He pulled out his phone.

"No need to call for help yet," I said, flashing an ace bandage and a Sam-splint. I also swallowed a couple of Advils and took a sip of water.

"Dad, I'm checking the Forest Service website. There's a fire around Saddle Junction.

We have to get out of here pretty quick."

"Yeah, how far are we from the fire road?"

"The contour map shows we're several miles away with all the switchbacks, but if we take that deer trail we passed, it's probably not more than a mile."

The tall grasses were flattened along a foot-wide trail heading west through the forest. I knew the area. "It will be a steep incline," I said. My son had taken off his shirt and was cutting it into large strips with his pocketknife.

"We can cushion these between the splint and your ankle bones," he said. "I'm fine with just a T-shirt."

"Okay," I said, folding the splint in half lengthwise. "If you stabilize my ankle, I can set up a stirrup, and we can bind everything tight with the ace wrap."

Ezra kneeled and grabbed onto my hiking boot to steady my ankle. "Let's hurry," he said. "The wind is picking up, and I smell smoke. I think we should use the deer trail."

After setting my foot inside the stirrup, I made a figure-8 bandage to hold everything in place. Ezra helped me stand and handed me my hiking poles. He had already put both of our packs on his back. I leaned onto my poles and limped forward. My son kept a slow but steady pace, not more than two steps ahead, always looking back to make sure I was all right. The trail was steep and narrow, but with his help, I got around boulders and climbed over fallen trees without stumbling. The wind had picked up, and the sky was a hazy yellow by the time we reached the fire road. Two firefighters greeted us. We quickly told them our story.

"Someone can drive you down to the trailhead," they said. "From there, you can get back to town."

Ezra called his mother to explain the situation. Minutes later, we climbed onto the back of a pickup truck and watched passing fire crews prepare their gear. A couple of airtankers flew overhead. Ezra was tapping on his phone again.

"Really?" I asked, "who are you calling?"

"I'm texting." His fingers crossed the keyboard faster than I could breathe. Then he looked at me and smiled.

"And?" I said.

"Cleo's not pregnant, Dad."

My Sixtieth Birthday

"She's not too young for you," my sister joked as she took her seat at my table on the patio, "you're too old for her."

I was only mildly embarrassed that she had caught me watching the swaying hips of a young woman exiting the coffee shop.

"Well Jenny, I may be old," I said, "but I'm not dead." I forced a laugh, but she had put her finger on a source of my bourgeoning depression.

"Sixty's not so bad, is it?" She squeezed my arm tenderly. It was several years already since my divorce, and my life was measured not by years but by events: college graduation, starting my own company, marriage, the birth of my children, and a tumultuous love affair with the wrong woman. Now my best friend was dying from cancer. Part of me wanted female companionship — if only I had the courage to date.

"Always looking for that next adventure," she declared.

If only she knew that I was struggling with a lack of confidence to perform. No one had prepared me for this; neither my father, nor my uncles, and certainly not my little sister. Starting today, these were the real sixties, and I had to own up to the sexual dysfunction of my older years. My testosterone had plummeted; my desire for sex vanished, and even pleasuring myself was a burden. When I looked in the mirror, all I saw was a chubby, balding old man with sparse gray hair and drooping shoulders. The crow's feet and irreverent pout formed by permanent wrinkles at the corners of my mouth made me feel grossly unattractive. Gone for good were those days when I could draw a woman's eye with my mischievous smile.

"I feel invisible," I said, "like a ghost, you know? I might watch these girls, but they're all so young, and besides, no one sees me anymore. If it wasn't for an occasional conversation with a waitress here at the coffee shop, I'd shoot myself."

I was surprised to see Jenny raise her eyebrows. She didn't smile when she said, "That sounds pretty grim. I hope you're joking."

I bit my tongue. Men like me don't share their feelings easily, especially with family.

She nudged my shoulder. "Are you okay?"

"I'm tired of all the shaming language used in those commercials touting Viagra and testosterone-boosting supplements," I said. "Women have menopause, right?"

"And men have andropause," she said. "We're all affected differently, but it's inevitable."

I sensed a finality in her voice, so I decided to drop the conversation, and asked her to update me about her own life.

"My mammogram is clean," she said. "It's been three years now since the chemo."

"Yay!" I didn't tell her about my elevated PSA, or about my visit with the urologist. "Two older guys at the climbing gym shot themselves last month. Rumor is they were happy. They had good retirement incomes and successful careers."

"You never know what is going on inside a home." My sister was a psychologist. "Maybe they couldn't handle ageing, or their loss of physical strength and stamina, or maybe they were having family issues."

"Sounds like a poor excuse for suicide."

"Guys kill themselves with increased frequency these days. There's a wave of clinical depression drowning teenage boys and older men in this country, and the government's not doing a thing about it."

"Not every sixty-year-old is depressive," I said.

"Maybe not, but andropause is real, and men tend to crawl under a rock and deny it until it's too late."

"I have low testosterone, and I can't get it up." There, I said it, and strangely, I was proud to have upped the ante of our conversation. "What do you have to say about that?"

She chuckled. "I'd say that telling someone you have low testosterone is probably not the wisest thing to share on a first date."

I didn't find her comment amusing. She could probably tell because she quickly changed her tone and sounded serious.

"Have you thought about taking supplements?" she asked. "A girlfriend of mine says testosterone gel changed her husband's libido and his mood. Strangely, she's not that happy about the increase in their sex life. Many women our age aren't into sex that much anyway."

I shrugged. "I'll be okay."

She put her arm around my shoulder. "I'm concerned about you," she said. "I love you."

We spoke for a while about various things: books we were reading, and holiday plans, and about our kids. Several women my age and older came and went through the coffee shop's doors. But none captured my attention. Regardless, I felt like a dog that couldn't bark.

Jenny must have noticed my foul mood because she put her fingers at the corners of my mouth to pull my cheeks upwards. A forced grin crossed my lips.

"Now, you're smiling." She laughed.

I replied half-jokingly. "As they say, life sucks, then you die."

"And like you said when I got here, you're not dead yet," she countered.

Her words rang home like an epiphany, and I felt glad that I had shared a piece of my saddened self with someone who cared so much about me. A pretty young thing had shimmied onto her chair at the far end of the patio. She crossed her slender suntanned legs and brushed her long auburn hair away from her eyes. I marveled at her femininity, and in the throes of malevolent evocations accompanied by my genetically programmed urge to multiply, I fondly reminisced. Photographs of girlfriends past scrolled before my eyes as her nimble fingers tapped across the coffee shop's lunch menu.

I saw my sister frown, but it was a playful grimace, one that I had often seen when we were growing up together. She had noticed the object of my distraction. I felt inspired.

"Hemingway once won a bet by crafting a six-word story," I said. "It was, 'for sale, baby shoes, never worn'."

Jenny raised her eyebrows. "And so?

"So, maybe I need to change my life. My story should be live now, eat ice cream, and play."

She wrinkled her forehead and pouted. It reminded me of my mother. "That's seven words," she said.

I couldn't restrain a laugh. "Indeed, it is, Jenny. Indeed, it is."

The young woman at the other table wore strands of turquoise beads around her wrists. Her hair had settled wildly on her shoulders, but I could tell they matched her teardrop earrings perfectly. A pair of dragon tattoos graced the length of her forearms. I marveled at the audacity with which her generation tackled body paint. I smiled, and when she smiled back, I felt excitedly alive, grateful that my heart could feel the glorious remembrance of it all.

Alone

I'm alone in the patient compartment of our rig, separated from my driver, who's also an EMT. He can only hear me through the thick glass window. The ventilator fan is set on high, just like we were told to do after the World Health Organization declared the Coronavirus a pandemic with fatal repercussions. We've been out since six this morning. I just chucked the last disposable gown in our emergency kit, and I've been wearing the same N95 respirator mask for three days now. Three 12-hour shifts, three days in a row, but I consider myself lucky. Friends of mine just have surgical masks, which we know provide no protection. Funny how some bosses suckered us into thinking they did some good, and besides, they said, what else are we to do?

The 60-year-old diabetic woman we just picked up is pasty-looking and wheezing. Her daughter claimed it was a bad asthma attack and she was out of inhalers, but when we called it in and said the gal's got fever too, they told us it's probably the virus.

I double-check her oxygen mask. Her breathing is getting worse, and she can't talk. I take another blood pressure reading—it's low.

I can't feel a pulse.

"What did the dispatcher say?" I shout to my driver.

"It's a forty-five-minute wait at the ER, and we're still ten miles away!" he yells back to me over his shoulder.

"We're screwed," I mutter under my breath, knowing he can't hear me anyway with the sudden yelp of our siren and the screech of our tires on the road.

"I'm giving her a breathing treatment." I holler. He needs to know what I'm doing.

"That's against regulations, remember? No nebulizers in infected patients. It might spread the virus."

"Well, those were guidelines—we never got a written order. Besides, I don't know if she's infected, and she sure as hell doesn't have COVID-19 positive tattooed across her forehead."

"You're gonna get us fired."

"Just drive," I say.

I break open the nebulizer bag and prop the woman up on the gurney. For a moment, I think she's looking at me, but then her pupils roll up under her eyelids, and her eyes go white. "Damn, she's coding." I jam my fingers over her carotid and can't feel a beat. A lead from the electrocardiogram monitor falls off. I start chest compressions. The rig lurches forward. I can almost feel my driver leaning on the accelerator.

"Let her go," he shouts.

"I'm not giving up no matter what the boss might say." I tear off my fogged-up goggles. "Maybe it's not the virus, maybe. . ."

She perks up. She opens her eyes. I reconnect the EKG lead and see a waveform.

She's alive.

We pull up to a special entrance of the emergency department. The doors swing open. A doctor and two nurses wearing hazmat suits start dragging the gurney out of the rig.

"What happened?" the doc says, not taking her eyes off my patient.

"Just an asthma attack," I say. "Nothing more."

"You sure?" she says. I can tell she sees the nebulizer. I can tell she knows. I swallow hard.

"I'm sure." We've got another call. I'll file the paperwork when we get back.

"Stay safe," the doctor says, pointing at my goggles before swinging the vehicle door shut, "and..." but the rest of her words drown in the wail of our siren as we take off.

Serengeti 101

"Oh, God!" Rashel's outstretched fingers clawed at the gnarled bark of the baobab as I pounded her against the tree's colossal trunk. I gazed upward through its leafless branches, tapered like the fractal anatomy of a human airway stretching into the sky. Not two feet away, quite oblivious to the teenager's screams, a hoard of siafu, the vicious red Army ants of East Africa marched single-file toward their unsuspecting prey in the distance.

"Don't stop," she said. "Wait, no, no... stop." She wiggled out of my grasp and slapped her hands onto my chest, pushing me away. "It's too much," she laughed. "Time out. It hurts. You have to stop."

Seeing her flushed cheeks and the way her melted mascara darkened the skin around her eyes made me smile. "You look like a hyena in heat," I said.

"And what would you know about scavengers?" she said. She leaned against the tree and pulled on her panties, pink, with little white flowers that stood out against her dark skin. "Or maybe, Hmm..."

I hadn't told her that I won her by drawing straws at the embassy in Dar es Salaam. Nor that I bet we would have sex in each of Tanzania's national parks. This was trip-day number four, and we were still in Tarangire. With several days to go and only three more parks to visit, my chances were looking good. I pulled up my trousers and looked around. "Your shorts are here, somewhere," I said.

"Aw, now aren't you an Eve-teaser."

She sounded serious, so her words softened me like water in a warm jacuzzi. I didn't take her homespun Indian-English euphemism for sexual assault lightly. "This was consensual," I ventured. "Wasn't it?"

"Let's put it this way," she said. "If my dad were here, he would not be happy."

Now I was worried.

"But…" Then she broke laughing. "He's not here!"

"Jesus, girl, don't do that. You had me scared shitless."

"Yeah. That's what you get for telling the old man to let me come with you on safari. Oh, don't worry, I knew I could handle all four of you."

I never knew if it was the wine or the sustained euphoria from chewing too much khat that evening, or maybe just the shock of having almost died from Dengue fever, but when I first met Rashel at the embassy, I was mesmerized. Within seconds I lost any sense of decency that could have prevented me from seducing an eighteen-year-old.

Truth is, my friends were not evil in a criminal sort of way; they just had non-controlling superegos. Frog was the oldest. He was a surgeon who had been bumming around combat zones on the African continent for years. Jack was a humanitarian aid worker who collected women craving brief, life-changing experiences. He's dead now...caught a stray bullet in Rwanda during an uprising. Thomas was a year older than me. He was a professional rock climber and wingsuit fanatic who had just tested HIV positive. He slept around without taking precautions even after his diagnosis. He's dead too, but not from AIDS. I think he got hit by a bus in Cairo or something. Anyway, I told Rashel I ran black market gemstones through East Africa. She didn't care to know much else. Besides, she didn't think the sixteen years between us was that big a deal anyway. It was only twice as much as between Bogart and Hepburn in The African Queen, she said.

So, I asked my friends to put in a good word with her father, the ambassador. Rashel had just arrived from New Delhi, and he thought seeing animals on safari would be good for her. The five of us could share my Toyota Landcruiser, I said. It was already packed with enough food for an eight-day trip, so I knew there would be plenty of opportunities to court her, but I didn't tell him that. I mean, my friends were going to say something after our bet, but they were drinking too much that night.

After leaving Tarangiri, we were rumbling across the savanna when I told her. My friends were leaning out the windows to escape the Tsetse flies, and with the cacophony of the Landcruiser, they couldn't have heard anything anyway.

"Next stop is Lake Manyara," I said, "unless we drive straight on through Ngorongoro Crater to Olduvai Gorge in the east. Then we can enter the Serengeti through the Naabi Hill Gate.

She didn't seem impressed.

"Rashel," I said, getting her attention. "I won you in a bet, and we have to have sex in every national park." Her eyes opened wide, but at first, she didn't say anything. I marveled at the way her hair was dyed a raven-blue that matched her painted fingernails. I closed my eyes, and for a moment, I remembered the red butterfly tattoo that garnished her left ankle, now covered by her low-cut hiking boots she was still wearing barefoot. When she spoke, her British accent was marked with cute colloquialisms she had picked up while living in India.

"I won't act pricey," she said, popping into my arms to kiss me. That meant she wasn't going to play hard to get. Her cut-off jeans were short and tight. Her small rump and plump but inviting thighs begged to be fondled. She whispered into my ear. "It does sound kind of exciting," she said. "I mean, sex on safari, just a one-of in every camp." She pronounced *of* with an f, rather than with a *v* sound like the rest of us would. "Where do we club it next?"

I had never heard the expression.

"You know, get together." She laughed hilariously as she climbed over my knees to squeeze into a space the size of a jerrycan between me and the window. Her hand was wrapped tightly around my biceps as we began bouncing around like unsecured luggage. My friends were still talking, so I could hardly hear her speak into my shoulder

"In all seriousness," she said, "and it's true.

"What?" I said, incredulous.

"Yes, until a moment ago." She said it again. "Until a moment ago, I was a virgin."

Some things are beautiful, I thought...simply beautiful and timeless, like a baobab, or the wildebeest, and even the zebra herds that migrate to the Masai Mara along the western corridor of the Serengeti.

Eve's Night Out

The desperation in her voice haunted him during his rush through Saturday night traffic, and Logan's thoughts raced as if he were driving into the scene of an old pulp movie. He had told Eve it was too late to go for a run, but she was stubborn, and a marathoner. He admired that, but he never liked the way she could be gone for hours pounding the pavement by herself.

He burned red lights and illegally crossed lanes, passing dozens of vehicles in his haste. Before making a sharp turn into the old church parking lot, he was jolted by a speed bump. The area was dark except for a street lamp a hundred feet away. Eve's half-dressed body was slouched against the decrepit shell of a Metro booth near the lot's entrance.

He pulled up in front and jumped from his car. His wife was naked from the waist down. Her light running jacket was ripped, and her sports bra had been pulled around her neck, exposing her breasts. Her head tilted limply to one side like an abandoned rag doll with rolling eyes. Her forehead was covered in blood.

Please God, he prayed silently. Scrambling toward her, Logan noticed shreds of gray acrylic fabric from Eve's running pants strewn about on the pavement. Her light green headband lay in a puddle of vomit next to her cell phone. She was barefoot, and he never saw her sneakers.

When he knelt beside her, he retched, shuddering at the sight of her cracked lips and broken front teeth. Her cheeks were bruised, and her right eye was swollen. He knew the jagged laceration stretching from the corner of her mouth down to her chin would scar her forever. He hoped the punch hadn't broken her jaw. Wiping fresh tears from her face with his shirttail, he engulfed her body in his.

Eve's face was expressionless in a sad, absent sort of way. Her body was cold and limp as if any strength she might have mustered to resist the onslaught had suddenly been drained from her. She didn't seem to be looking at him, but rather through him, as if she were gazing emptily into the starless night.

Her voice was broken and raspy. "Get me out of here," she whispered.

He wiped his fingers across her swollen eyelids and tucked a few locks of disheveled brown hair behind her ear. He tried to pull her onto her feet, but she didn't have the strength to stand. Her neck disappeared into her shoulders from the effort, and she collapsed like melting wax onto her knees.

"I've got you," he said, lifting her again with both hands under her arms. She was heavier than her thin, 5-foot frame suggested, but he was able to carry her to the car. He leaned onto the hood, bracing himself as he reached down with one hand to open the door. She moaned when she crumpled into the passenger seat. A streak of blood dripped from between her still uncovered thighs, and there were bruises on her shins and small porcelain feet, as if she had been kicked and stomped upon. He reached across the headrest to pull a plaid woolen dog blanket from the back and draped it over her shoulders. Folding the blanket around her, he covered as much of Eve's shivering, mostly naked body as he could, trembling when he wiped what was probably dried semen from her chest.

A few passers-by were gathered near the parking lot. They seemed to move cautiously toward the car, but with curiosity, not to offer help. Their undulating movements in the shadows of the nearby street lamp reminded Logan of dancers in a scene from West Side Story. Suddenly, like fish swarming in expectation of a feeding frenzy, they began running toward him.

"Let's go," Eve pleaded.

He closed the car door and darted to the driver's side so he could slide behind the wheel. When he turned the key in the ignition, his headlights blinded the crowd. Backing away from the curb, he struck an orange traffic cone that bounced onto the adjacent greenbelt.

"We need to get to the hospital," he exclaimed, putting the car into forward drive. His words bounced off the windshield and hung heavily in the claustrophobic space.

"No," she mumbled.

"You're hurt, Eve. We're going to the hospital, and I'm calling the police."

"Just take me home. Please, just home."

He sped onto the boulevard, undecided whether to turn toward the hospital or go left to their house on Central Avenue. Eve vomited over the dashboard well before he reached the intersection. He immediately stopped the car and held her in his arms.

"I'm so sorry," he told her over and over. But his words, although ageless, felt insignificant.

§

DEATH

Can time reverse itself like a roll from a slow-motion camera?

Unanswered Questions

"I'm done with this!" Brittney threw her cell phone out the window of her pepper-white Mini Cooper and reached over her shoulder for the colorful cotton beach sack in the back seat. A tube of lip gloss, a bottle of clear nail polish, and a handful of candies spilled onto the carbon-black leatherette when the bag caught on her headrest.

"Shit," she raged, missing the entrance to the freeway. She leaned forward to wipe her windshield, squinting to see through the fog. On most days, the old reactors of the San Onofre nuclear power station stood out like a pair of implant-filled breasts on a beach-decked California girl. Today, they were barely visible in the haze.

"Fuck 'em," she muttered. Slamming her foot on the accelerator, she yanked on the steering wheel and sped south down the northbound exit of the interstate.

Visibility was especially poor along that stretch of the Pacific Coast Highway. Drivers had their headlights on, and outside temperatures ran five degrees lower than usual. Hovering clouds covered the road like mist in a Hollywood horror film, and a steady drizzle rattled over her windshield like tumbling hail on a glass-paned roof.

A passing car honked annoyingly. Britany flashed her middle finger at the driver and made a sharp right turn at the bottom of the exit lane, intending to join the other vehicles on the freeway heading north. Her back wheels slid over a pool of water as she fishtailed into speeding traffic. Had the stereo not been blasting, she might have heard the screeching tires of a Chevy Silverado trying to avoid rear-ending her.

Brittany wasn't wearing a seatbelt, but the truck's middle-age driver was. The Silverado hit the back of her Mini Cooper full force, sending the small car flipping over a metal barrier into a ditch. Its front wheels spun aimlessly as remnants of the crushed automobile stood erect for a moment in the mud. A pacific pocket mouse scrambled out of its nest and crawled up the mangled front fender, then jumped into the sagebrush while mayhem continued on the adjacent road.

The Silverado was hauling a 24-foot Airstream trailer that jack-knifed against the rear of the truck when it struck Britany's car. Ripped off its hitch, the Airstream spun into another lane, where it smashed a blue Toyota Prius carrying a forty-two-year-old father of three. A white Mercedes slammed into the Prius, shoving it over the rear of a mother's Mustang. Her two kids were crushed like paper cups in the backseat seconds before the rolling, tumbling trailer flattened all three vehicles to smithereens.

Drenched in the smell of urine and feces, the truck driver may have lived long enough to feel warm blood from a ruptured artery drench his pants. First responders said he died struggling to free himself from the grip of his safety belt. Its buckle was stuck against the center console, and they couldn't cut their way into the cab fast enough to save him.

Two days later, a California Highway Patrol officer found Brittney's phone by the side of the road. "I never want to see you again," was typed in bold capital letters across the backlit screen, but no one discovered why.

Kate Can't Fly

"Don't leave me!" Kate's shout stops me at the curb. I look up to see her climb over the railing of our third-floor balcony. She holds on with both hands, toes flexed over the rain gutter, arms fully extended behind her. Long brown hair tumbles onto her breasts when she leans forward.

I'm crying, but now I'm angry too. "What the fuck are you doing, Kate?"

"You're the liar, remember? You promised not to leave!"

This is pure manipulation, like her cutting, and even the kinky sex. I don't take my eyes off her. "Kate, I'm sorry."

"Sorry? You're a joke."

There is desperation in her voice, but it's from desperation that I left. I couldn't take the insults, the blame, or the walking on eggshells any longer.

I remember the Alprazolam.

"Did you take anything? Did you take those pills?"

"Yes, all of them."

I'm in the street. People around me are watching.

"Stop this foolishness," I say, "I'll come back upstairs." I don't care that my sense of self-worth is shot. I should walk, but it's an addictive relationship.

"You always say I'm foolish."

I know the dance. This is just another conversation going around in circles, but Kate's sleeveless Bodycon mini is high on her thighs. Pretzel-stick legs shine with baby oil and sweat from our recent love-making. She's not wearing panties.

God, I love this girl, almost as much as I love the craziness of it all. "Get off the ledge, babe."

She dangles her right foot in the air, mocking me.

I raise my voice. "I said, get off the balcony. Now!"

As she leans out further, I find her perversely attractive. No matter how often we fight, I'm like a junkie—I can't break away.

Her toes never leave the edge as her weight pulls her forward. She hovers, her eyes widen.

Jesus, no.

It's a swan dive.

Fifty-thousand thoughts rush through our heads every day, but as Kate lingers, mine are for a moment suspended. Her slender outstretched fingers won't stop the air from moving between them. My shirt ruffles in the sudden breeze, or maybe I'm shivering. Can time reverse itself like a roll from a slow-motion camera? I imagine my girlfriend back on the balcony, but a bone-cracking thud smothers my scream.

A Cold Little Secret

It is -30°F, and a transcendental winter sun pauses briefly on the horizon. Fred and I are tracking polar bears near Barrow, more than 300 miles north of the Arctic Circle. Alone and almost invisible in our cream-colored 4-wheel-drive Toyota, we are beyond the icy shores of the Chukchi and Beaufort Seas when a dense curtain of fog forces us to retreat toward the haven of the city.

Struggling over a steep incline, we fishtail into a snowbank and flip onto our side. My slightly dazed friend grabs some rope and a chainsaw from the back seat before clambering onto the snow. I check myself for broken bones and squash the queasy feeling in my gut, then follow him up and out the driver's-side door. Biting winds burn my face and bring tears to my unprotected eyes.

Obeying Fred's instructions, I secure our rope to the axles with a couple of hitches, keeping a double-length free. He carves a thick block of ice from the frozen snowbank on the other side of the road, chopping in a few grooves to prevent the rope from slipping when it tightens. My exposed fingers are shiny and numb by the time we wrap the rope around the block and back to the capstan winch on the hood.

"Damn, it's cold." My breath freezes over my collar when I exhale. The wind whistles sullenly through layers of power-stretch fleece covering my ears, and my thumb is turning blue from early frostbite. I shiver when my neck muscles tighten, a sure sign my brain has ordered surface capillaries to constrict.

The crunch of Fred's boots disrupts the death-like silence fluttering across the frozen plain. He slides into the driver's seat and starts the engine. The capstan turns continuously until the truck begins to list. With a muffled thump, we are on all four wheels again. I jump in and close the door, struggling to unzip my jacket before burrowing aching fingers, hard as tootsie rolls, into my armpits.

"Happy day," my friend shouts after tearing off his ski mask. His handlebar mustache is white with ice. He turns the heater on full blast, and we roar over the snowbank. Fred's mother was Inupiat Eskimo. His father worked in the oilfields north of Fairbanks. Coming home after Operation Iraqi Freedom, Fred left the Marines and settled in Barrow to become a hunter. I struggled another year in Special Forces, then drifted back to San Diego. Support from other vets helped, but I couldn't get my act together. I figured it was time to hit Alaska for a visit.

"Let's hope that doesn't happen again," I say.

"It's like in the war, dude, but we're lucky."

"I'm glad you had the chainsaw."

"Never leave town without it or my rifle."

I wipe condensation from the frost-covered windows to admire the dusky landscape, then stick my hands back inside my jacket. "It sure looks different from Southern California," I say.

Fred explains how sheets of ice collide over constantly moving oceans, piling into jagged pyramids called pressure ridges. They remind me of the concrete barriers we built to prevent car bomb attacks in Bagdad.

He points to a heap of five-gallon paint cans on a nearby trash dump. "Keep your eyes open," he says. "Bears think there's food in those honey buckets."

"What honey buckets?"

"This time of year, it's dark for ninety days and colder than hell, so whenever the pipes freeze, people crap in their cans and leave them here till summer."

An arctic fox darts across the frost-covered road and melts into the polar twilight, invisible except for its short black ears and muzzle when it turns to stare. Our headlights catch a glimpse of gold in the fox's eyes before the animal vanishes into the wilderness.

We skirt the Heritage Cultural Center and drive south toward an area nicknamed Satellite City. A steel-gray forest of parabolic antennas the size of shipping containers points horizontally across the low horizon. A metal research hut stands high on stilts above the tundra. Except for a snowy graveyard garnished with a dozen crosses, the barren landscape of the arctic desert stretches on forever.

"Permafrost starts just below the surface." Fred nods toward the cemetery. "We can't dig deep, so we build mounds on top of the graves."

"We didn't bury anyone in Iraq, remember?" The scorching heat sucked moisture out of enemy bodies till they turned into parchment-covered mummies. Aeolian winds and sand did the rest.

"Kids launch their snowmobiles off those mounds." Fred stops the truck in the blue-tinged shadow of a cluster of crosses. He keeps the engine running.

I pull my hands from my jacket. It's as if a jackhammer is pounding on my heart. This can't be happening. I blink my eyes to chase away memories devouring my brain.

"Maybe I should build a fence around those graves." Fred's words echo far away.

My throat is swelling—I can hardly breathe, but I won't panic. PTSD is bad enough, and I don't want my friend seeing me this way again. I muster a few words. "Hell, when you're dead, you're dead."

Shit, I need to piss. I squeeze my thighs together, but a few warm squirts leak into my crotch. I'm trembling, squirming around. This car seat isn't big enough. Tears are going to freeze on my eyeballs.

Fred pounds the steering wheel before grabbing me by the shoulders. "Don't go there, brother. Get a grip."

"But he was a kid!"

"We thought he had a grenade, remember?"

"He was still writhing after I shot him."

"We didn't have a choice, okay?" Fred's bellowing voice smothers the growl of our engine. Small icicles fall from his eyebrows. His massive palm is wrapped around the nape of my neck as he shakes me reassuringly. "We're alive, aren't we."

He floors the accelerator. Our tires spin wildly before gripping the icy road.

"But he was just a kid, and we dropped him in a shit-pit!"

Fred shrugs, like it's our little secret.

Too Late for a Kiss

Julie stretches across the spacious king-size bed to open the book on her nightstand. Tarnished petals of a dried carnation mark the inside cover. Pencil scrapings huddle like ants on pages where her husband underlined sentences and made undecipherable scratches.

"I left an envelope with all my papers on the desk," he said when he called from the airport. "If anything happens, there is life insurance."

As usual, she scoffed at his fear of flying. "Nothing is going to happen."

"The car is in the parking structure. I sent you the receipt."

"The miracles of modern technology." She squelched a laugh.

"I'm glad we paid off the house, and with my pension, you'll have enough for the rest of your life."

"Darling, I'm not worried about the rest of my life." She didn't say it had been the same refrain on every business trip.

Julie remembers his sweat-soaked palms the night they were married. He was nervous, he said, but someday they would go on a honeymoon. After the ceremony, they strolled hand-in-hand from City Hall to the bus-stop. They stopped at a bar to escape the rain. It was happy hour. They had two beers for the price of one and food was on the house.

The book is about keeping a marriage alive.

"It's a good read," he said before leaving. "We'll talk when I get back."

She slipped his favorite necktie into his suitcase. Dinner conversation was politely warm.

He climbed into the taxi.

She was surprised when he called again at 4 am. An ominous purple glow seeped between the bedroom's curtains.

"I'm sorry to wake you, but I can't sleep," he said.

"And I thought you finally felt guilty about seeing a younger woman." She was only half-joking.

"I wouldn't call about that. I'm in my hotel room, and I have the most terrible headache."

"You're having a lot of those recently. We should see a doctor when you get back."

"I'm sure it will be better in the morning."

"Call me if you feel worse."

"I will. Thank you."

"Bye."

"Bye."

Forty years, one word.

Whisper Red

Clunk. The small, red camping stove dropped onto the granite ledge between the climber's feet, then rolled to sit upright against his right ankle. It was only a few inches wide and weighed less than a pound, but the sound was heard a hundred feet below.

Jack manteled his way onto an oven-size rock. He was proud of how stubbornly he could press his hands down onto its flat surface, then lift his knee to his chin before sliding his body onto the platform like a beaching whale. He looked up at his climbing partner, waiting at the anchor.

"Not elegant," he said, catching his breath. "But effective, right?"

"That's all that counts, dude, that's all that counts." Earl was an experienced mountain guide. He knew the importance of positive reinforcement for building confidence in younger climbers.

Jack hooked himself into a sling attached to the cams wedged in a crack, then doubled his protection by attaching another carabineer to a piton anchored to the rock face. He readjusted his harness before leaning back against the granite slab.

"Did you hear that sound?" he asked.

Earl was already flaking the rope into a neat pile at his feet. "I think the guy on the ledge up there dropped something."

Jack eyeballed a lone, bare-chested climber crouching on another ledge about a hundred feet above. He had a small backpack, but no rope. "I don't understand why anyone would climb without a rope," he said. "It's no different from stupid men challenging each other to a duel in the 18th century."

"Alexander Hamilton and Aaron Burr weren't exactly stupid."

"What I mean is, there is no good justification for climbing without a rope. Magazines say it's for the adrenaline rush of dying if you make a mistake."

"That sounds about right," his friend said.

"You mean you've free-soloed too?" Jack was torn between admiration and thinking Earl was a fool. "I've never told anyone. It's something I do sometimes, you know. There's no epic or anything." "What if a hold broke off?"

"Then it would be the longest couple of seconds in my life."

Jack took a few hexes from his friend and hung them on his gear loops. Next stop was the ledge where he had glimpsed the other climber.

"It's an excuse for suicide, I say, no different from dueling or Russian roulette."

Earl looked surprised. "Didn't you ever climb a tree when you were a kid?" he said. "You did that without a rope, and your parents probably thought you were crazy."

Jack shoved a partially crushed energy bar into his shirt pocket. "Yeah, maybe. But stupid is as stupid does."

"Climbers aren't stupid. We know what we can do—we trust our technique."

"Well, it doesn't matter how good you are. Just one unlucky break and you're dead." He tightened his figure-eight knot and prepared to climb.

A sky-splitting scream made him jerk his head around. Instinctively, he grabbed for the shadow of a bare-chested man cartwheeling past him, but there was only air.

Then silence.

Lots of silence.

Earl was hugging the granite rock face, one hand clenched on the anchor. "He almost knocked me off the fuckin' wall," Earl yelled.

"Holy shit!"

"You didn't think you could catch him, Jack, did you?" "I don't know, for a minute, I thought. . ."

"There was nothing you could do."

Jack noticed that his partner's knuckles had turned white. Earl was grasping the anchor like he was holding on for dear life. "Jeez," he said, "he just flew past us."

"What do we do now?" Jack watched his friend pull a bandana from his back pocket. Earl had pissed on himself. "His eyes were huge," Earl stammered, "like he was surprised."

Jack couldn't look down. "I think he was holding something. Did you see it?" "I saw everything, man, but it happened so fast. I'll never forget it."

"What happened?"

"He dropped his stove." "What?"

"That sound we heard—must have been his stove. Maybe he fell when he picked it up, or maybe he slipped."

Jack shuddered. "I could have stopped him." His throat was swollen, and his heart pounded inside his chest. He inhaled deeply to hold back tears—to keep his mind from going elsewhere.

"You couldn't have stopped him," Earl said, "I mean, you reached for him, I saw it, but it's not like that scene in Cliffhanger. He would have pulled us both off. It's that terminal velocity, 32-feet-a-second-squared thing. He was going forty miles an hour."

Slivers of cirrus clouds lingered in the neon-blue sky. Jack saw people gathering far below, at the base of the cliff. "We should go down," he said. "I'm not sure I can climb anymore."

"Chalk up, man. We'll top out in two; then we can walk off. It's safer for us to keep going."

The sudden confidence in Earl's voice made Jack reconsider. Rock climbing was a dangerous and unforgiving sport. Maybe that's why he was addicted to it; to the way it made him face fears, he would have never known he had.

The two friends hugged. "Are you ready?"

"Yeah."

Jack watched as Earl double-checked their knots and verified the anchor's strength. All the carabiners were locked. "Belay on," he said.

"Climb ready." Jack reached for a small jug. "Climb on."

The young man transferred his weight onto a dime-edged irregularity and pushed himself off the ledge.

Kansas City Ganges

Loren died last week. He was hiking to the summit of Pyramid Peak, a fourteen- thousand-foot climb in the Elk Mountains about 12 miles west of Aspen, Colorado. According to friends, a rock gave way under his feet, and he plummeted down a vertical slope into an inaccessible gully. When I heard the news, I closed the shop and contacted my colleagues at Search and Rescue. A helicopter had spotted his mangled body at the bottom of a cliff, but there was nothing they could do to save him. I loaded my gear and left Boulder immediately.

It's been a year to the day since Loren invited me to dinner in Kansas City. Remembering the evening better than a sports commentator remembers the blow-by-blow of a heavyweight prizefight, I ran our conversation through my head as I drove past fields carpeted with wildflowers on my way to Pitkin County.

He'd taken a phone call from his doctor.

"Finally," he said that evening, "an explanation for my nausea."

I had graduated from college and was spending time with my maternal grandparents in The Walnuts, an upscale apartment complex near The Country Club Plaza, not far from Loren's hotel. They knew him since his teenage years when he and my father aggressively courted my mother. My grandmother didn't like him.

We didn't see Loren much while I was growing up, but my parents spoke of him often. My mom told me stories about his travels, his mountain climbing, and his catastrophic amorous adventures. "He'll never settle down," she'd say, but she looked happy when he was around.

My father was killed in a car accident when I was sixteen. Loren stepped in like a godsend to help us settle into a small apartment my mother could afford. He lived in Colorado, but he visited us in Kansas City almost every month. Sometimes, he spent the weekend in our spare bedroom. I hoped my mother would marry him, but that wasn't in the cards, and six years later, just before college graduation, she was diagnosed with metastatic breast cancer and died. It happened pretty fast.

I was caressing the pink ribbon on my jacket's collar when Loren picked me up in front of the sports store window on Ward Parkway. It was an early summer evening, so we skipped a meal at Zoë's Kitchen and hopped a cab to the River Market, an area of shops and eateries south of the banks of the Missouri.

Loren beckoned me into an Indian restaurant with beige stucco walls and a dozen tables covered with immaculate white linens. A dark-skinned man wearing tuxedo pants and an embroidered shirt smiled and bowed. His teeth were white as the table coverings.

"It is good to see you again, sir," the maître d' said to Loren.

"Thank you. It is good to be back."

"You were traveling, sir?"

"Yes," said Loren. "The Himalayas again, and Colorado." He put his arm around my shoulder. "This is my young friend and business partner," he said. "He'll soon be joining me in Boulder."

The man bowed his head and clasped his palms across the front of his chest in a typical south Asian greeting. "Good evening, sir." His eyes lingered on my face.

"Good evening," I said. I turned uncomfortably to Loren. "Business partner… Boulder? What do you mean?"

"I mean that you can leave Kansas City now. You're good with numbers. You could manage my outdoor gear shop in Boulder and still have plenty of time to climb. Don't think about it. Just say, yes."

I was flattered. Loren had one of the most successful mountaineering shops in Colorado, but I didn't think I could leave Kansas, yet. After all, I had just finished school, my grandparents were aging, and my mother died only months before.

Besides, he said he was ill. A chill went down my spine as I thought about it. Other than my grandparents, I was closer to him than to anyone. For a moment, I felt like an orphan. I restrained a melancholy smile—like an orphan with a gear shop.

The maître d' floated on the balls of his feet as he led us to a small table in the corner of the restaurant, far from other diners. He pulled a chair from under the table and motioned me to sit.

"We are blessed that Mr. Loren brings his son to our humble establishment," he said in a muffled voice.

"What?" I said.

But he had already made his way around the table to Loren. He draped a large white napkin over his knees and returned to my side wanting to do the same. I ignored him and spread my napkin on my lap. A busboy filled my glass to the brim.

"Your father is a good man," he said, tilting his head toward Loren.

"He's not my father," I whispered.

The busboy smiled as the maître d' discreetly backed away to greet other guests. A waiter wearing a turban appeared at our table.

"Good evening, sir." He offered me a choice of leather-embossed menus written in Devanagari or English.

"Good evening," I answered. "I'll take the menu in English please—thank you."

"You are very welcome, sir. Thank you, sir." He clasped his hands in front of his chest and lowered his eyes. He turned to Loren. "Good evening, Mr. Loren, sir. Would you like the usual?"

Loren seemed captivated by a corpulent blond with overdone make-up and a garish dress complaining about overly spiced food at a table nearby. He took his eyes off her for a moment and nodded. His long gray hair was unkempt, barely covering a bald spot on the crown of his head. He shuffled his chair to make room for the busboy who replaced our white china plates with two finely crafted wooden bowls. The waiter centered mine in front of me, its rim perfectly aligned with the round edge of the dining table. I pushed it away from the edge, closer to my silverware.

"Loren's son should visit his father more often," the waiter murmured. His head bobbed side to side after he leaned forward to speak into my ear.

"I'm not his son."

"But a father should not be alone," he whispered. "Only a son can spread his father's ashes in the holy river."

"Holy river?" I wasn't sure I heard correctly. I turned to look at him. "We're in Missouri…You mean the Ganges, in India?"

He leaned toward me again, but I could barely hear him. "Yes, of course, sir. Only a son spreads his father's ashes in the Ganges. It is a man's duty."

I stirred in my chair and looked at my host. "Loren," I said, "I don't mean to be rude, but could you please tell this man I'm not your son?"

Loren chuckled.

"You really should visit your father more often," the waiter insisted, his voice slightly louder now. He repositioned my bowl against the edge of the table directly in front of me. I pushed it back a few inches to where I had placed it before.

The man stretched his long fingers to delicately put the bowl at the edge of the table again. He cupped his other hand to his mouth as if he wanted to share a secret.

"Nothing is more sacred," he said.

"My father died when I was sixteen," I said. I wanted to tell him my mother was dead too, but I feared the tension in my voice. I pushed the wooden bowl away from the edge of the table one more time and took a sip of water.

The busboy appeared from nowhere. The waiter pushed the bowl in front of me. I felt like a guest on a comedy sitcom.

"You are very blessed," the busboy said.

I looked across the table. Loren seemed lost in thought, but the waiter was showing him something on the menu.

"Loren?" My voice broke. Why did I feel like crying?

"Yes, son, what is it?" Loren lifted his eyes.

The waiter's head wobbled side to side as if the reply had justified his every word.

And it did.

Jungbu's Mother

"Three nips and a cup." The shapely owner of the Himalayan teahouse smiles after filling my reusable marmalade jar with chang for the second time. I take three sips, and according to tradition, guzzle all that remains of the sweet barley wine. An empty plate of Dal Bhat lays next to my plastic lawn chair, not two feet from a cast-iron stove in the center of the room. The Nepali dish of steamed rice and lentils did little to calm my churning intestines.

"Chang better than dal for upset stomach," the owner says. A lock of black hair thicker than a yak's coat covers her face when she leans forward to pour another glass. She brushes it behind her ear with a flick of the wrist and picks at her silver loop earrings. This time, she doesn't wait for me to drink, but returns to the kitchen, pausing to remove a dish from the golden oak table in the main room. A Tibetan wool carpet with blue floral designs covers a bench under the window. Rugs that used to be hand-woven are now machine-made and synthetic, purchased in bulk from China and carried by mule, yak, or human porter to the most remote regions of Nepal.

"She's beautiful," I whisper to Mingma, the Sherpa mountain guide sitting next to me.

"Yes," he says, "but she is sad."

The owner is peeling potatoes. She is small, maybe fortyish with broad shoulders and slender hips. A full-toothed smile stretching between high cheekbones ignites her brown complexion. Her face radiates health and intelligence. She doesn't appear to be sad.

"My uncle gave her this place after her husbands died," Mingma says.

"Did you say husbands—as in many?" I turn my head to follow Mingma's gaze toward the wood-paneled wall behind me. A jumble of signed photographs is tacked next to a portrait of the Dalai Lama.

"She comes from a region in Tibet where women have two husbands," Mingma says. "They are usually brothers. This way, the property stays in the family if one of them dies."

"So, she is Tibetan," I say.

"They were my cousins. They died on the mountain."

"What do you mean?"

"They climbed Makalu." Mingma points to a large color photograph of climbers smiling on a snowy ridge of what is the fifth highest mountain in the world. "There was a terrible accident," he says, "and now she is alone."

"Who is the kid?"

"The young boy outside making dung paddies? He is Jungbu, her son."

I look at the owner again, this time with curiosity and admiration. She is humming a Nepali folk tune as she adjusts a weighty pair of drapes that prevents cold air from leaking through the door into the teahouse. I wonder what it was like for her to sleep with two men, and if she knew which of them was Jangbu's father.

Mingma pokes my arm. "Many years ago, his grandmother—her mother, was killed by Maoist insurgents not far from this valley. It was near Ngozumpa glacier, on the trail to Gokyo Ri."

"My God, I know the place! My guide told me about it last year when we camped there." I sip my chang, forgetting my glass is empty. Not wanting to ask for another drink, I study the old photographs. Several are of Sherpas who climbed Mount Everest. Some dirty expedition tee-shirts hang near a vertical row of Tibetan prayer flags. Mingma and I are the only guests.

The owner's son comes in, leaving a track of mud on the tiled floor. The aura of hardship is palpable now, made even more acute by my newfound awareness of his family's history. I feel insignificant—I am insignificant.

The little boy strains to lift the stove's cast-iron top with a pointed stick. His mother adds a handful of junipers to the coals. She pours some kerosene and drops in a dozen shriveled paddies of dried yak dung. An odor of freshly cut grass and lighter fluid, combined with the sudden heat, makes us back our chairs away from the stove. Feeling queasy, I unzip my down jacket and stuff my wool cap in my pocket.

I am still harboring symptoms of altitude sickness after failing to climb Ama Dablam. Avalanche risk from heavy snowfall, and intestinal problems, forced me to descend from high camp three days ago. Now that I am at a lower altitude and in the warm haven of a teahouse far from the trekkers' highway, I feel cowardly, wondering why I hadn't mustered the courage to summit.

Ama Dablam, means "Mother's necklace" in Nepali. They call it that because the 6,857-meter peak is protected by two long ridges that surround a hanging glacier the way a mother's arms might cradle a child, and because the glacier has the shape of a dablam, the traditional pendant worn by Sherpa women. Far lower than Everest and its neighbors to the north, the mountain is a stunningly steep pyramid of ice that captures the gaze of anyone traveling through the Khumbu valley.

I had quit my job, and for two years, I had dedicated myself to climbing. I read books by mountaineers and world-class athletes for inspiration. I finalized my divorce to rid myself of harmful emotional baggage. I exercised daily to improve my speed, stamina, and strength. But, I was fifty years old and a relative newbie. My friends said I couldn't do it. Ama Dablam was no 8,000-meter peak, I told them, but it was my Everest, and like every hero, I would surmount any obstacle preventing me from my goal. I scaled Kilimanjaro and volcanoes in Mexico and Ecuador. I climbed Ben Nevis in the winter. I even trekked twice to Everest base camp before making a solemn ascent of 6,200-meter Lobuche East. Mistakenly, I thought I was ready.

Mingma raises his glass in a toast. He's smiling. He must sense a need to interrupt my negative thinking.

"To Ama Dablam," he says.

I touch my empty glass to his. "To Mother's Necklace."

The owner of the teahouse offers us more chang. I study her naturally full lips, ruddy cheeks, and twinkling, slanted eyes. A small, turquoise-laden jewel box dangles on a silver chain around her neck. It teases my chin when she reaches over my shoulder to pour my drink.

"You like her, don't you?" Mingma grins like a schoolboy.

"Very much," I say, "but like the mountain, she is beyond my reach."

Mingma speaks before drinking. "Only a madman pursues impossibilities," he says.

I wonder if we are toasting the mountain or if this forty-year-old veteran of the Himalayas just paraphrased Marcus Aurelius? I quote the philosopher-king myself. "How ridiculous to be surprised by anything in life," I say.

"Life is what our thoughts make it," Mingma jousts.

"And you, my friend, are a wise and learned Sherpa." The clouds over my heart lift miraculously. I lean toward the stove and raise its lid with a juniper branch, emptying my glass onto the coals. The sudden hiss makes the owner lift her eyes from the plastic bowl in her lap to look in our direction.

There she is, crouching now with her back against the wood-paneled wall; a widowed Tibetan wearing blue jeans, gold Adidas running shoes, and a tight-fitting red fleece jacket; a woman raising her son alone in the high mountains of Nepal, with no company other than an occasional band of crusty mountaineers.

I pull up an empty chair. "Come, join us by the fire."

She shovels a handful of rice and dal into her mouth. Jungbu sneaks out from behind the curtains. His mother pushes the youngster forward with a pat on his butt. He offers us a handful of sweets, then sits playfully at my feet.

Mingma sticks out his tongue the way Tibetans stick their tongue out in greeting.

Jungbu's laughter makes me smile.

"Maybe," Mingma says, "Ama Dablam is not so bad after all."

When the owner brings us ginger tea, she is carrying three glasses.

Never a Coward

Ain't no sense dabbling with these jugs any more. The janitor tossed the bag of artificial holds into an army surplus storage locker and forced his grey, weather-beaten face into a closed-lip smile. He stared at the dark, irregularly-shaped blotch on his forearm.

Fucking metastatic skin cancer. He put his hand reassuringly on the Glock 9mm pistol in his pocket. Again.

A few scraggly-haired young men were battling gravity on the gym's climbing wall. The janitor tugged at his silver ponytail, remembering he was once like them, with straining biceps and cut-off shorts that showed off his muscular thighs. It was funny to think that in the '60s, his testosterone-fueled exuberance was legendary, like a vortex clamoring for attention from climber groupies grazing at Yosemite's Camp 4.

Men of his generation didn't play at being brave in the luxury of a climbing gym. They gathered under the granite domes of Tuolumne Meadows, planning multi-pitch ascents on vertical walls. In the evenings between cigarettes and beer, they cuddled with their girlfriends, wearing Tie-Dyed shirts and sharing beta from their climbs. When they weren't listening to California bands like Steppenwolf, The Doors, or Credence on the radio, they heard news about other men their age fighting in Vietnam, more than seven thousand miles away.

In April '68, around the time Royal Robbins soloed the Muir Wall, Khe Sanh was the deadliest battle of the war. Walter Cronkite, also known as the most famous name on television, spoke up against the fighting. People took to the streets while students protested on college campuses. Those who weren't chasing degrees got married to avoid the draft, and many fled to Canada. The janitor, whose father fought in World War II, decided to join the Marines.

He actually looked forward to the unavoidable reality of combat.

Thinking there was no better way to prepare for battle than to rock climb, he dropped out of college and spent a year cheating death on his own terms. He was joined by a draft-dodging friend who had also spent time in the valley. They dreamed of following in the footsteps of climbing greats like Norman Clyde, Eichorn, and Harding. Packing a rack of carabiners, pitons, a hammer, and a rope, they sent routes at Stoney Point, then drove to Tahquitz and the mountains around Idyllwild. He grew tired of his friend's trepidations. So, inspired by the way Tom Bauman rope-soloed the 3000-foot face called *The Nose* on El Capitan, he chose to climb alone.

He loved the way his forearms burned when he risked a prolonged pinch on a sandstone knob. On granite, he pulled precariously on two-finger pockets, letting his legs hang free before a stretch to the crux. Sometimes, his superhuman efforts made him groan like a prehistoric man before the invention of language. Other times, he celebrated success with chest-pounding roars and pumping fists, his muscles flared with exaggerated sexuality that seemed anything but ephemeral.

His Samson-like long hair and flowing adrenaline made him believe he was ready for war, but he confused recklessness with bravery. Whatever attitude he had would be lost in the claustrophobic jungles of the remote A Shau Valley, just thirty miles south of Khe Sanh.

The ambush occurred near a military encampment called Fire Support Base Ripcord. The sudden cacophony of deadly machine gun fire made even the toughest men wet their pants. The wounded scattered wildly with soul-piercing screams that cut through the hellish, lurid smoke. Explosions from a thunderous rain of enemy artillery shells were enough to blow out a man's eardrums. The impact of a 7.62mm bullet from an AK-47 spun him around dizzily. A mortar blast knocked him off his feet. The soldier he'd been speaking with lay dying in the ditch next to him, his mouth open as if he were shouting.

Blood was everywhere.

One of his buddies, eviscerated and writhing like a disemboweled fish, landed with a thud on top of his chest and shoulders. After he clawed himself out from underneath his friend's body, a switch flipped from arrogance to fear in the 20-year-old's mind.

I can't die like this. I've got to get out of here.

Clouds of shrapnel smothered the air above his head. He retched violently, then dropped his gun in the dirt and crawled away, thrashing through the vines and deep jungle grass. He ignored his comrades-in-arms who were hopelessly setting up a defensive position using bodies, branches, and anything else to protect themselves from the onslaught. A medic found him hours after the firefight; a lone survivor burrowed deep under the torched wet earth; buried among the dead; whimpering and wounded, rolled up like a baby and howling aimlessly inside his bloodied field jacket.

The janitor wiped the sweat from the treadmills. *And I thought that would be the worst of it.*

He bitterly recalled the challenges of rehab and his prolonged stays in a VA Hospital. It didn't matter that he had PTSD or was seriously wounded, or that he was spit on and called a child-killer when he got back from Vietnam. What mattered was that he survived while others hadn't. Haunted by the specter of cowardice, he spent the rest of his life on the harshest of mountains, because no matter how reckless he could be, climbing would never feel anything like war.

He looked at the young men on the gym's climbing wall, wincing at the way they one-upped each other. It reminded him of the time he roped up with a stranger on the Regular Route of Yosemite's Higher Cathedral Spire. He was weak from chronic pain, but acting strong, he took the lead. He never heard his partner's warning about fractured rock and peeled off an easy hold during the 5.9 traverse on the second pitch. By the time the guy caught his fall, he had slammed into the rock, breaking four ribs and puncturing his left lung.

Despite the blow to his reputation, climbing gave him reasons to go on living. He also learned that both life and death were inevitably unpredictable. Maybe that's why he didn't like watching kids goof off on the wall, especially when they topped out fifty feet from the ground and leaned back without warning, trusting whoever was tied to the other end of their rope to hold the fall.

His fiancé rappelled off the end of hers on some worthless peak near Chamonix. He never heard her scream.

I can't believe I let that happen.

He slouched in a corner and buried his face in his hands. Tears welled up in his eyes. He never trusted himself with anyone after that. Traveling the world to climb more or less alone, he soloed Uganda's Mountains of the Moon and labored through icy winters on Ben Nevis. He built a name for himself writing magazine articles, but he didn't share his personal stories, and he never talked about his fear.

He looked around the gym to be certain no one saw him cry. Nodding graciously to the reverent head-tilt of a young stud he once coached, he emptied the trashcans, scraping his forearm, then shuffled toward the bathroom. *Not everyone can be a hero*; he wanted to warn the young man, thinking the fellow was old enough to abandon any delusions of immortality.

He locked the door.

I've been volunteering here for years, so why in hell can't I stand people watching me clean crap from a toilet bowl.

He pulled the Glock G19 from his trousers and put the barrel against his carotid artery. He pointed the gun toward the top of his head and looked in the mirror. The blotch on his forearm was bleeding.

For some reason, he remembered crashing headfirst into a granite slab on Cerro Torre a decade ago, in the Southern ice fields of Patagonia. Although he wore a helmet, the fall broke his jaw and split his head open enough to need twenty stitches. He never heard the shower of snow that pelted him off the wall a dozen feet above his last cam.

His partner was the 20-year-old son of his friend from his climbing days in Yosemite. The boy must have wanted to protect himself from the barrage of ice suddenly pummeling him from above. He surely hugged the wall in desperation as he kept the rope from rushing through his ATC, and maybe he heard the hollow sounds of cams popping one after the other. When the rescue team arrived, the youth was dead, crushed by a block of ice. His brake hand was locked on the rope, and his steadfast belay saved the man's life.

The loaded magazine was in the janitor's shirt pocket. He pulled the gun away from his jaw.

Not today, he thought. *Not today.*

Sarah's Lesson

Sarah put her hand on my forearm and dug a fingernail into my white coat. "Doc, I druther you not call my husband in just yet," she said.

"Doc?" I smiled. "You never call me doc." I finished installing the morphine pump and set the dose at an hourly rate. The intravenous line fell like a noose from a bag of saline slung above my patient's shoulder.

"I just need to be sure I have your full attention."

Her southern drawl sounded almost comical. I knew she was exaggerating to make a point. "He wants to be here," I said, "when it's time."

Sarah ran her tongue over her chafed lips. "I've told my family everything I had to say. The kids are all grown up. My husband is too. They'll be all right."

"I'm worried he won't understand." I tried to imagine how he felt, alone in the hallway outside the room.

"It's called letting go, my friend. It's Buddhist." She propped herself up on her pillow and pulled the bedside table near. I almost spilled her water cup when I pushed it within her reach. She would not have wanted me to hand it to her.

Sarah squeezed my forearm as if she read my thoughts. "You can handle it."

"I'm not sure." I looked at the wall clock over the door. It was well past midnight. Everything was ready for surgery in the morning, but our plans had changed.

"My husband will understand," she said. "We've talked."

"Sarah, just hours ago, you wanted to keep on fighting."

"Y'all mean *you* wanted to keep on fightin'. I don't recall saying so." She grinned weakly before taking a sip.

The fluid in her chest had returned. The x-rays showed there was a new intestinal blockage, and her pain was unbearable despite narcotics. Earlier in the day, I advised surgery to keep her alive and arranged for a private room in the hospital. She called me after dinner.

"Henry, it's time," she said.

The palliative care team was out of ideas. Living three years with several metastatic terminal cancers was already a miracle.

Sarah's hands shook as she put her cup on the table. We were on a first-name basis since our first meeting. She said I reminded her of someone. Her eyes closed. I pulled the bed curtains in a vain effort to lessen the noise from the hallway. The rattle startled her.

"Where is everybody?" she said.

"They are outside," I whispered.

Her closed-mouth smile bewildered me. She had the same smile when I first confirmed the metastatic nature of her cancer years ago. Her symptoms began while vacationing in Paris, and being a physician, she immediately sensed the diagnosis. She was in the church of Saint-Germain l'Auxerrois, she told me, a stone's throw from The Louvre. The church was built from a mixture of Gothic and Renaissance styles. Her vivid description of its stained-glass windows and tower bells made me forget how thousands of Protestant Huguenots were massacred there by French Roman Catholics in 1572.

"It's where I met the love of my life," she confided later. Naively, I presumed she meant her husband.

"My goodness no," she said coyly. "I mean my French lover, my youth, everything I could have been."

I'm not sure why, but from that day onward, we bonded. Just as strangers might unexpectedly become intimate travel companions, we shared our life stories without the typical reservations that inhibit most doctor-patient relationships. When I bragged that I had learned to connect emotionally with my patients, she scolded me. Your desire to understand others is commendable, she said, but it's meaningless as all get out unless you first discover your humanity, and that is the work of a lifetime.

Our chats were long conversations that caused delays in my clinic and prompted reprimands from the administration. I didn't care. I dreaded our many encounters because they meant she was ill, yet I looked forward to them, guiltily.

She never talked down at me despite our forty-year age difference. Nor did she discuss her family, work, fame, or any of her well-known scientific discoveries. Instead, she shared her love for painting and early twentieth-century art. She could recite the Rubaiyat of Omar Khayam as prolifically as the poetry of Robert Penn Warren and Wallace Stevens. The way she told me she almost dropped out of medical school to become a sculptor made me think I was listening to someone writing a novel.

"Promise me somethin'," she insisted months later, after yet another palliative procedure. I was discharging her from the recovery unit. She couldn't button her blouse. The simplest gesture had become difficult after rounds of chemotherapy left her once dexterous surgeon's fingers insensitive and clumsy. Her breathing was labored. Her abdomen uncomfortably distended. She couldn't eat without being nauseous, and pain killers blunted her ability to think. Dying was also living, she remarked. It's all part of the adventure.

"You must promise me," she said, "that when the time comes..."

I tried to interrupt, but she put her fingers to her lips.

"Now, hush your mouth," she ordered. "Give me your word that you will turn up the morphine, gently, so I don't wake up."

That was not a request, I thought. Her decisional powers were unquestionable. I was intimidated, but her strength of character was inspiring. I remember nodding affirmatively, but it was a devil's bargain, and today was pay time.

I felt uncomfortable standing over her. Stupidly, I folded my arms. I quickly dropped them to my side. "Your call this evening was unexpected," I said.

She patted the quilt she had brought from home and motioned for me to sit beside her. Her closed-mouth smile had a warmth I hadn't seen before. "Isn't it always?" she said.

"I have you on the morning schedule." I was desperate.

"I am sure you do," she said. She tugged at her nightshirt under the covers, then struggled to button her collar with trembling fingers. "But we have an agreement."

"Yes." I helped her with the last button.

"So, let me tell you a story about the love of my life."

I swallowed hard. The room was bathed in a grey, cold light from fluorescent bulbs. I didn't know what to do with my hands, so I folded them in my lap. I felt like a model in one of Modigliani's paintings.

She put her hand back on my forearm. Her drawl was musical. "We met at that same church I done told you about before. He wasn't religious mind you, but he liked serenity. He was a short fella, muscular, with bright eyes just like yours, and black hair thick as a mop. Lookin' at him made me laugh, but I'm tellin ya, when he looked at me, I thought I saw the secret of life itself."

She paused to breathe. Her lips quivered. "I figure it took us an hour to jaunt up the hill to Montmartre, and by the time we passed that monstrosity called the Sacré Coeur church, I was in love. We bought fruit and bread at the market, and yes, fresh eggs-for the mornin'. He told me his name, it was a king's name, and I drew his portrait while sitting under a cherry tree that overlooked all of Paris. It was like something out of a movie. We even lived in a garden apartment near Picasso's old place called the bateau lavoir on the Rue Ravignan. Soon enough my poor neck was covered in passion marks, and a few days turned into a year."

She put her thumb and two fingers to her lips, smacking them. "L'amour," she said, smiling the way the French smile when the wine is good, and a delicious meal is over.

"What happened?" My question stuck in the air.

"Reality. I didn't have the gumption. I fled. I returned to New Orleans and medical school. Eventually, I found another man and bore his children."

She glanced at her feet under the bed covers, as if studying her position, then raised her chin. She squinted and furrowed her brow while I fought back the tears, trying to restrain my emotions.

I wanted to say something meaningful, but I was tongue-tied and sputtered something foolish.

"You've helped thousands of people."

She waved my words aside. "Well, bless your sweet heart. That means a lot."

I heard the door open. Sarah's husband pulled the curtains and quietly kissed her on the forehead. He sat in the corner of the room, saying nothing while she slept.

An hour passed.

"How do we know she wants to die?" he whispered.

I was still sitting on Sarah's hospital bed, watching her heart rate fall. The seconds lingered between breaths. Her body was beaten, but her eyes were steadfast when she opened them, though she seemed surprised each time she emerged from her slumber. When I saw her close-mouthed smile again, I knew she had made her decision.

"It's your first time," she said.

"I nodded."

"We always remember our first."

I swallowed hard again. My eyes were burning.

"Let's do it," she said. She nodded faintly before pushing the back of her head into the pillows. I released the lock on the intravenous line above her shoulder, causing the liquid to flow faster through the plastic tubing. Sarah waved at her husband and put her hand back on my forearm. She winked. "I'll see you on the other side."

A Death in Quito

Elisa and I meandered between churches on the cobbled streets of the sleepy Ecuadorian capital. She described her work with Bolivian immigrants in Argentina, while I complained about logistics in Venezuela. Exhausted and breathless, we also spoke of times when Spanish conquistadors oppressed indigenous peoples throughout Latin America. Now, we were in Quito to help with sanitation planning in the poverty-stricken slums called *barrios illegales* on the outskirts of the city.

Neither of us had adjusted to the altitude yet. A wearisome uphill jaunt took us past sun-dried brick and stucco-covered houses built in the old Moorish style. Elaborately-carved wooden doors opened onto manicured central gardens dominated by eucalyptus trees whose medicinal smell reminded me of California. Gazing up at a vast interior balcony that towered over checkerboard stone-tiled patios, I thought of our last travels together, providing shelters for flood victims near Elisa's home in Santiago, and medicine to community clinics in Brazil. She was a friend, but our relationship was guarded. We had even slept together once, perhaps as an experiment, the way friends have sex to test the waters, but nothing more.

After reaching a restaurant perched high above the city and far from the traditional tourist track, we feasted on Chilean Cabernet and Seco de chivo, a goat stew served with yellow rice and fried plantains. The elderly owner, himself an Aymara Native Bolivian from the region around Lake Titicaca, colored our imaginations with elogious tales about Antonio José de Sucre, who, under the command of Simon Bolivar, freed Quito from Spanish domination in 1822.

We began the downhill walk to our hotel shortly after midnight. A plump old woman with thick braided hair and a skirt covering her ankles struggled past us up the steep incline. A brown felt hat tilted precariously off the back of her head, almost touching a bulging, dark plastic garbage bag attached to her knapsack which, almost twice her size, hung bandolier style across her stooped shoulders.

Step after halting step, she shuffled, grasping her hands together at her waist as if she could lean onto them to pull herself forward. Balancing the load on her back and panting, she paused to breathe. Her chest was almost parallel to the ground, her coarse woolen shawl dangling from her back like a blanket on a pack animal. Unexpectedly, she straightened her spine and stared not at her feet, but at the cobblestone pavement ahead as she heaved herself into the empty air in front of her in order to renew her calvary.

She lost a sandal and stumbled. Her distorted body spasmed and stretched sideways when she crumpled to the pavement. Her hat tumbled into a garbage-filled gutter. Except for a twitch of her right hand, she lay motionless under a street lamp where a sign indicated the altitude, 3333 meters. A crowd rushed toward her from a nearby food stall.

We were less than a hundred feet from where she fell, but I could tell she had stopped breathing. An old man crouched beside her. His dark fedora, blue poncho, and white cotton pants suggested he was from Otavalo, an Andean village in the northern highlands. His long gray ponytail swooped past his shoulders as he lifted the woman's head onto his palms. A glowing cigarette dangled from his partially closed lips the same way the woman's tongue hung lifelessly from the corner of her weather-beaten face.

Her saliva drooled onto the pavement. A trickle of blood oozed from her ear. Her shawl had fallen aside, uncovering a multi-colored shigra bag made of agave fibers. A sudden gust of wind scattered a cluster of coca leaves from a tear in the woman's garbage bag. They littered the street, alongside excrement from passing dogs who stopped to defecate on the curb nearby.

"Malditos perros!" The old man's shout scattered the strays. A tall, obviously foreign woman pounded her cell phone, probably calling for help.

Elisa and I continued our walk. I shortened my steps.

"We should have done something," I said.

She hesitated. "Her destiny was to die in the street, my friend. There was nothing we could do."

"I cannot believe you just said that!"

Elisa shrugged. "What you believe or do not believe is of no matter. What is important is how you live, not where you die."

"You are tough," I said. I couldn't help thinking about why the woman carried coca leaves in a garbage bag. Where had she come from? With a stranger's curiosity, I looked back up the hill.

"She is with God now," Elisa whispered.

"That's interesting, coming from a nonbeliever like you."

"Such words are the only consolation for those who die."

I paused to look at her. "But you don't believe in God. Are you saying you would change your mind if you needed Him?"

Elisa avoided my glance and stepped cautiously over some dimly lit cobblestones. "I am saying, and we talked about this earlier today when we visited the Jesuit monastery in old Quito…"

"La Compania," I interjected.

"Yes," she said, without even a glimpse at the old woman or me. "God is a necessary fabrication—a universal truth that is real for almost all of us."

"But it is dishonest to presume God's existence only when it is convenient."

"Dishonest, yes. But harmless."

We reached a small terraced ledge protected by a waist-high wall of bricks. Nearby, a dizzyingly steep wooden staircase was fixed into the hillside. I stared out over a sleeping city, whose electric lights now brightened only the neoclassical dome of La Catédral, a sixteenth-century Catholic church built with rocks carried by slave-laborers from the nearby volcano Mount Pichincha. Elisa leaned on an iron handrail.

"I never told you," she murmured, "that along with my youth, my dreams, and my only lover, I lost God in the torture cell of a Chilean prison years ago."

She grabbed my elbow with one hand and placed her other on my wrist. There was tragedy in her eyes, but her body felt like a feather on my arm as if the heaviness of her revelation had miraculously been lifted from her shoulders. Her forward motion insisted we resume our descent.

"I am not sure that you lost God," I ventured.

She sighed. "You are still thinking about that woman, aren't you?"

I nodded with some embarrassment.

Elisa let go of my arm and nudged me in the direction of the stairway. "So," she said, "with or without God, she did not die alone."

The Colonel's Daughter

The pudgy-face, middle-age camp leader dropped a canvas tent bag at my feet and shook his finger in my face. "The girl is off-limits," he said. "Her father is a high-rank VIP, you got it?"

"Yes, Sir." I stood up straight and nodded.

"She will be staying with us until he is back from Iraq," he said. "Maybe a couple of days." *She*, he explained, was the only child of a US fighter pilot.

I threw the heavy bag over my shoulder. "I'll get her tucked in, no problem, Sir." I was there to help set up camp for military kids before starting summer school, not to babysit some colonel's daughter.

I pitched the tent on a wooden platform near the gravel-covered kitchen space our cook called a mess hall. He was a tough ex-Army Ranger, but he helped me make the place nice. We cleared a path across the gravel and lined it with flowers planted in a row of combat helmets. Then we built a wooden A-frame and hung a tarp over it.

I filled a three-gallon plastic jug with water and slung it upside down from the top.

"There you go," I said when Miss VIP walked over. "There's no hot water, but at least you can shower without stripping in front of a bunch of kids."

"Great," she said, with an edge in her voice. She was cute, lean, and lanky like a tomboy. She wore khaki cargo pants, with a light brown tight-fitting hiking shirt tucked-in. A nylon-web belt kept the pants up around her waist, and a camouflage-patterned buff covered her forehead like a bandana, leaving a handful of wavy brown locks over her shoulders.

Seattle grunge played from a loudspeaker in the kitchen area. I checked to see that my boss was gone.

"Do you need help with anything?" I said.

She opened the tent flaps and dropped her duffel bag inside. "How about setting up my cot?"

I unfolded the cot and sat down. She began unpacking her sleeping bag.

"The bag will fluff up more if you leave it out to air," I said.

"Yeah, I know."

"My boss says I'm not supposed to talk with you."

She rolled her eyes. "The man's just following my dad's instructions."

"Sounds protective."

"My father has been uptight since my mother died. He forgets I'm eighteen."

I leaned forward. "Sorry about your mom. Mine died when I was a kid."

"I'm Jamie."

I told her my name and how I was going to summer school before leaving for the Air Force Academy. Jamie kneeled on the floor and pulled hiking gear out of her bag. "My mom was a flight nurse before she got sick. She hated that my dad flies combat, but, he's Air Force too, you know?" Then she threw off her bandana. "Agh," she said, pulling a comb from her back pocket. She spent a minute easing the knots from her hair.

"The cook is making chili and rice for dinner," I said.

Jamie rolled her eyes again. "It's probably that dehydrated slop they serve in the army, right?"

"It actually tastes pretty good."

"Will he give me a beer?"

"If you promise you won't tell anyone—he likes breaking the rules."

She stopped fussing with her hair. Her eyes widened. "What rules?"

"Yesterday he threw a rake at some kid who walked across the kitchen area. He treats the place like it's his castle."

"What happened?"

"Nothing. He said he would kill anyone who complained."

Jamie shrugged. "He must be a Ranger." Her hazel-brown eyes gleamed as she ran her tongue over her upper teeth. She pocketed her comb and uncapped a tube of lip balm. A sweet raspberry smell filled the air. I could almost taste it.

I smiled and felt stupid.

"Want some?" she said.

Maybe she likes me, I thought. Our hands touched when I took the tube from her outstretched fingers. A black elephant-hair bracelet was wrapped around her wrist.

"It's real," she said, dangling her forearm in front of my face. "My father gave it to me before he went off to kill people."

"Is it worth anything? I mean..."

She got to her feet and handed me the bracelet. "The two knots stand for love and fertility."

Jeez, I thought, but I didn't say anything.

*Black hole sun, won't you come...*Chris Cornell's lyrics groaned from the loudspeaker.

"I love that song." Jamie waved her arms over her head with the rhythm. I had a tingling in my stomach. I was still watching her when the song ended.

"I'm so hungry," she said.

"I'll tell the cook."

"Will I see you later? Maybe we can talk."

I nodded and handed her the bracelet.

"You can wear it for a while," she said. She stuck her head outside the tent. "No boss in sight, it's safe."

We shared a fist bump.

I spoke with the cook, then walked a quarter mile through the woods to my campsite. I devoured a chocolate bar and fell asleep in my tent. It was dark when I woke, but I figured she was waiting, so I pocketed my headlamp and crawled out, taking care not to wake anyone. I followed the trail to Jamie's tent and crouched in the shadows.

Nothing like breaking the rules, I thought. Then I scratched the canvas. "It's me." I immediately felt foolish. Like, who else could it be?

"It's pretty late." She sounded drowsy.

I inched closer to the tent. "I'm really sorry. I dozed off."

"Wait, I'm putting on my shoes," she whispered.

Trouble is as trouble does. The truth is, I have no idea why Jamie wanted to see me, but I wanted to be near her. I took her hand, and we made our way silently up the trail, halting here and there in the dark to talk. I think she kissed me first.

We reached a small clearing between two storage bins. I kicked away a few plastic bottles that were lying in the dirt.

"You're shivering," I said.

Jamie tucked her chin into her Navy-issue turtle neck sweater. Her back was against one of the bins. I leaned forward to trap her playfully between my arms.

She clasped her hands behind my neck and smiled.

"You're beautiful," I said. Wrapping her in my arms, I kissed her. I felt the plastic Fastex buckle of her nylon military belt when she pressed herself against me.

My tongue ran over her lips. They tasted of raspberry.

"Hmm, slow down," she sighed. "This is nice."

We kissed again, but something rustled in the trees.

Footsteps. My boss's piggish silhouette towered before us. An intense light blinded me.

"And what have we here?" he barked.

"We're not doing anything!"

I was surprised by Jamie's outburst. Then, I felt bad for her.

The flashlight was still in my face. "Get back to your tents," my boss said. "We'll talk about this in the morning."

Jamie wiggled out from between my arms. We didn't kiss or say good night. Only our hands touched when I tried to hold her. Maybe she squeezed my fingers — I know she did. She bolted down the trail ahead of me and escaped into her tent. I put my head down and trudged back to my campsite.

It was six in the morning when I saw my boss staring at me through my open tent flaps. He was sitting on a plastic lounge chair, sipping his coffee, obviously waiting. I pulled my legs from my sleeping bag and rubbed my eyes.

"You're firing me," I said, thinking I'd be lucky if old pig-face didn't call the military police.

"Your girlfriend has got some bad news coming," he said.

I shook my head. "She didn't do anything."

The fat nose between his puffy, pink cheeks turned up as if he had pushed it against a windowpane. I felt him take my measure, and it was like knowing that someone has your life in their hands. Two guys wearing military dress uniforms and black armbands appeared at the trailhead thirty feet away. I blinked, and took a deep breath.

"The colonel was killed in action last night," my boss mumbled. "That's why I came looking for her. When I found you two lovebirds, I decided to wait until morning."

"Jeez, does she know?"

"Not yet," he said, rising to greet the men in uniform.

"Thanks, boss." I pulled on some jeans and a tee-shirt. I couldn't let Jamie hear the news alone.

Six Months and Counting

"I don't want this baby." Her thoughts became words that formed on her lips as she shuffled up the winding marble staircase to her apartment. She carried groceries in a brown paper bag in her left hand. With the other, she pounded a clenched fist repeatedly into her distended belly.

"I don't want you," she muttered.

She paused at the landing to catch her breath. Putting down groceries, she placed one hand on her hip and held onto the wooden banister with the other. She leaned her back into the railing. "I don't want you," she repeated, striking herself weakly again. Tears formed in her eyes. Then she let go of the banister and picked up her groceries.

When she stepped forward, her back foot caught under the fringe of the rug anchored to the landing. She stumbled awkwardly into the first step of the next set of stairs. Her head struck a marble baluster, but she was able to break the fall with her hand. As her body hit the ground, she felt her wrist crack. The bones in her forearm could hardly support the full weight of her body and the extra pounds she had put on since her pregnancy. Her arm buckled. Her groceries spilled onto the stairs. Beer bottles and soup cans clanked against each other chaotically before falling through spaces in the railing to the lobby below.

She stared at her distorted wrist and grimaced. "Shit." She felt under her dress with her uninjured hand and looked at her fingers. "No blood," she muttered. "Fuck, this is nothing like the movies." She struggled to her knees and rubbed her chin. Her tongue scraped against the jagged edge of a broken incisor.

Her thoughts were interrupted by an elderly man who stepped out from behind the door to his apartment. He hurried down the stairs to her aid. "Doctor, are you okay? You're bleeding," he said.

She looked down at her arm again. "I broke my wrist."

He dabbed her chin lightly with a handkerchief he had drawn from his pocket. "Your chin is bleeding," he said. His Eastern European accent was noticeable. "I shall drive you to the hospital immediately. My vehicle is parked directly outside. Please, let me assist you."

She wiped away more blood with her sleeve before grabbing his outstretched hand to help herself get to her feet. Her legs were wobbly, but she could support herself after draping her arm over the man's shoulder. When they reached the bottom of the stairs, he held the door open for her. She tried to slip into the back seat of his car, but she had gained so much weight it wasn't easy. She turned her body to the side and plopped down, but the momentum forced her to sprawl backward spread-legged onto the seat. She figured she had bruised her coccyx, and if it hadn't been so painful, she would have laughed. She lifted her legs and bent her knees while the man pulled her into the car from the opposite side door. He made sure she was comfortable, then plunged in front of the steering wheel and started the engine.

"Thank you," she said. "We can go to the hospital where I work. It's on the next block."

"Yes," he said. "I know it. Are you sure to be fine? Is there no damage?"

"You mean to the baby?" she said. "No, I don't think so."

He turned his head to look at her. "Ah," he said, "thank God."

At the Emergency Room, she received VIP treatment. She skipped the triage, dismissed the medical students and other trainees, and asked the nurse for a shot of morphine. Being a doctor came with privileges, she thought. The x-rays confirmed a double fracture, which the orthopedist on duty immobilized in a splint. He said that her ankle, which was quite swollen by now, was sprained and that her bruised tailbone was causing the pain shooting through her buttocks. He wheeled her into a private exam room where she lay waiting on a large recliner with her feet raised when her former husband walked in.

"Go away," she said.

She watched him shove his stethoscope into his coat pocket. He looked like he hadn't shaved in a week. "Are you okay?" he said.

She ignored the obvious. "How did you know I was here?" she said.

"They called me. I have an eighty-year-old on the table for a hip replacement, but I scrubbed out for a moment to check up on you. You'll need stitches on that chin."

"My tooth is broken."

"Yes, I see that."

"I don't want this baby."

"We'll get married again. All you have to do is say yes."

She glared at him, speechless.

"You should take some time off," he said. "Stay in bed for a few months, until the delivery. We'll get married after that."

"I told you I don't want it," she said again, as if the words themselves could make it happen.

He turned to shut the door, but she stopped him by holding on to the pocket of his white coat.

"You can leave now," she said. "Tell my obstetrician I'm here."

"Apparently, the dispatcher called him when you arrived," he said. He glanced at his watch. "I need to get back to the OR."

She pushed him toward the doorway with her good hand. "Yes, just go. I'll be fine." She watched him swagger out and put her hand onto her belly. "Why the hell did I sleep with him again," she whispered to no one in particular.

She'd been working double shifts. It was one of those miserable nights when the staff was frazzled after caring for dozens of trauma victims. They had called him to the emergency room for the third time. She was managing a patient in alcohol withdrawal. Until then, she had avoided him... in fact, she had avoided him for months after the divorce. But that night, they joked. They drank coffee, and they talked. He mirrored her perfectly, but she knew his reputation, and several nurses even told her they had slept with him. It was after midnight. She was on a break, and stupidly, she had followed him to his office where, somewhat to her surprise, she found herself kissing him.

To hell with romance, she remembered thinking as she stepped into the office. They kissed again, rather methodically. He shut the door and pushed her against the wall. But when she felt his weight on her shoulders, pushing her to her knees, she went willingly. Mysteriously, his surgical scrubs fell to the floor.

Boxers, not briefs – that's new, she thought. Looking up, she noticed him watching her. She didn't touch him with her hands but took him straight into her mouth. Pausing for breath, she looked up again.

"Fuck me," she whispered.

He lifted her to her feet and dropped her scrubs, panties and all before turning her. Entering from behind, he gripped her hair in one hand while trapping her around the hips with the other. Soon he was fully inside her, pushing her head downwards as if she were a jackknife. For a moment, she feared she might lose her balance. She didn't like it, but hearing him groan, she knew it would be over soon, and when it was, she turned her head and spun away from him. She watched him from across the room, thinking how ridiculously statuesque he looked, standing in front of her with his shorts around his knees and scrubs at his feet, with half an erection neither coming nor going, his penis dangling meekly between his legs. She quickly pulled on her clothes and grabbed a black elastic band from her breast pocket. After gathering her hair into a ponytail, she twisted it counterclockwise and holding it in one hand, wrapped the band around her newly formed bun until it was tight.

"I should clean up," she said, reaching for the door.

He looked surprised.

"I'll see you later," she remembered hearing as she stepped across the threshold into the hallway. "We can have breakfast together."

She answered, "yeah, maybe," but what she was really thinking was, *what am I doing?*

After that, she did her best to avoid him almost entirely. Four weeks later, the pregnancy test was positive.

She was sourly reminiscing when her obstetrician walked into the exam room. He was an older man in his early sixties. He had been one of her teachers when she was in medical school, and she had trained with him for a month before joining the hospital staff the year before.

"You could have lost the baby," he told her softly.

She didn't care. "I'm all right." she said.

He took her hand in his as he stood over her. "I think so, but we should do an ultrasound...and I would like to keep you in the hospital overnight if it's okay with you."

"That's reasonable," she said. "Thanks."

"Good," he said. "I'll make it happen."

She thought he was going to leave the room, but he didn't move. Instead, he pulled up a stool and sat next to her. He took her hand again in his. He delicately laid his other hand on her belly. There was a tenderness in his eyes she hadn't seen before.

"It's not like you...tumbling down stairs," he said.

"I don't want this baby anymore." She couldn't believe she had finally told someone. She felt her eyes become puffy as she held back the tears. "I know I'm over the legal limit, but I don't want it." She looked out through the window. An ambulance and a few parked cars were in the courtyard between two hospital buildings, and a lone maple tree had lost its leaves since the first frosts of autumn.

Going South

Jason could not help noticing her drawn features, the wrinkles framing her mouth, and her faded eyeshadow. He thought today should feel like any other winter day, no matter how different it may have seemed. His fiancé reached into her purse for a tube of lip gloss then stooped before sliding into the front seat.

"Thank you," Sarah said, lifting her feet onto the floor mat. A sweet cherry aroma filled the air around her. Jason leaned across the center console and gently pulled the car door shut. Admiring how she massaged the soft, waxy balm over her chafed lips, he followed her gaze through the windshield and out toward the oppressive shadows cast by the giant oak trees lining the clinic's poorly lit circular driveway.

They didn't speak, but he turned the key in the ignition and dropped his phone on the seat near Sarah's leather gloves and black Chanel purse. Driving past the parking lot, he pulled a piece of candy from his pocket and popped it into his mouth. He didn't think she could have any. Avoiding the cars lined bumper-to-bumper on Main Street, he was able to snake around the neighborhood's back avenues toward the freeway entrance miles away.

The night fell quickly, dark and serene. He leaned forward to turn on the radio, but thought better of it, and wrapped his hands back around the steering wheel. He stopped obligatorily at a traffic light. Red quickly turned to green.

"Go!"

Stunned by Sarah's outburst, he pushed his foot on the gas pedal and weaved his way into the crowded lanes of the Southern Expressway. Mostly lone drivers occupied countless cars. Many were tapping away on their cell phones.

"At this rate, we'll never get home," she complained.

Peeved, he turned his head to admonish her, but sensing some anxiety, he guessed there was no cause for anger. For a moment, he took his eyes off the road. She looked tired and older than her thirty-five years. He strained to find words that might soothe her palpable discontent.

"I don't like driving when it's dark," he declared, squinting from behind his eyeglasses.

"Would you prefer I drive?" The sharpness in her voice was an obvious hint that her question was rhetorical.

He reached across the console to put his hand on her knee.

"I'm okay," he said, "you shouldn't drive." He turned on the radio, finding a smooth jazz station. "Everything will be fine."

Sarah turned it off. "Yes," she said. "Of course."

They drove on in silence, neither able to ease the other's burden.

"Traffic is heavy," she finally offered. "It's Friday."

"Yes," he replied. "It's always deadly on Fridays."

"You're an idiot."

Jason winced but said nothing. For a while he eyed Sarah sporadically, and from the way she had buttoned her coat and double-wrapped the grey cashmere scarf around her neck, he knew she was cold. As he withdrew his hand from the steering wheel to adjust the heat, she began rifling through her purse. The high-pitched sound of keys clinking against loose change went on interminably.

"Did you forget something?" he asked.

Sarah stammered. "My wallet, I forgot my wallet." Her eyes swelled with tears. "I left it on the counter when I checked out."

Jason swerved quickly to avoid a passing eighteen-wheeler. For a moment, they were caught in the truck's blind spot. He raised his voice over the explosive rumbling. "I'm sure you have it," he said, clutching the steering wheel with both hands. He accelerated into an adjacent lane, narrowing his eyes to lessen the blinding glare of headlights in his rearview mirror. "Maybe I should stop," he said. "Do you want me to turn around?"

Sarah didn't answer. She was busy rustling through her purse with both hands. First, she dropped a Kleenex on her lap. Then she pulled out an atomizer of perfume, some folded papers, and a plastic pill bottle that she threw onto the dashboard. The pill bottle fell to the floor.

"Did they give you that at the clinic?" Jason asked.

"Obviously." She turned the roof light on and began hunting for the bottle between her feet. "Where did it go?" she muttered. "It must have rolled under the seat."

"You can find it when we get home."

"No, I'll find it now," she insisted, unbuckling her seatbelt and battling to find the lever that moved her seat backward. She unbuttoned the lower half of her coat. "Oh, my wallet is right here in my pocket." Waving the dark orange leather between her thumb and fingers, she dropped the wallet into her handbag." Could you slow down now, so I don't get tossed through the windshield?"

He backed his foot off the accelerator and watched her lean forward. She groped blindly beneath the seat.

"I'm sure it's under here, somewhere..."

Jason frowned. "Did you find it?" He didn't like Sarah to be without her seatbelt.

"Not yet," she growled. Her fingernails made a scratching sound on the rubber floor mat. "Okay, I've got it." She picked up the bottle and shoveled it into her purse with everything else.

"I don't feel well," she said.

Jason saw her lay the palm of her hand over her lower abdomen. "Are you okay?" He switched on the blinkers and maneuvered toward the outer lanes of the freeway.

"I'm not sure."

"Are you in pain?"

"Stop at the station. I need to get out."

He exited as soon as he could and pulled into a sparsely lit rest area, where he stopped the car alongside a series of trash bins competing for space. Without a word, Sarah opened the door, flung her purse over her shoulder, and stepped into a biting wind that slashed across the pavement and onto the front seat. She buried her chin into her coat collar and stumbled around the open door toward the front of the car, stopping to put one hand on the hood. With the other clutching her lower abdomen, she retched violently.

The overhead lamp went out when he pulled her door shut. He rushed from the car in time to catch her purse before she vomited. He gathered her long hair in his hands and pulled her scarf upwards. Trash littered the pavement in front of his headlights. She vomited again.

"I'm here," he mumbled.

She pushed his hands away and leaned her elbows on the hood, wiping her lips with the back of her sleeve. Then she coughed.

"I'll be fine," she said, stepping away. She took a deep breath and tugged at the waistline of her coat. Then, she retched.

"Really, do you think so?" Jason put his hands on her shoulders. "I can turn around. We'll go back to the clinic. It's not that far."

Sarah shook her head and wrestled free. "I'll be fine," she insisted.

"Are you sure?"

"It was my decision."

"You did the right thing."

"I'm glad you think so."

"You did. I mean, we did." He tried to wrap his arms around her again, but she slipped away before he could hold her.

"Please don't," she said, stuffing her hands in her pockets and hunching her shoulders. Sarah leaned her back against a trash bin.

"I need to pee," she said.

So, Jason stepped onto the curb and made his way to the back of the car. Waiting, listening, until the intermittent spatter of his fiancé's urine on the pavement ceased.

"There, I'm done."

She sounds exhausted, he thought. After walking through the gleam of his headlights, Jason crouched for a moment at Sarah's side. Rising to their feet together, he helped her back into her seat, but not before removing his jacket, leaning forward, and wrapping it diligently over Sarah's chest and shoulders. He closed the door. There was yet an hour's drive ahead before they'd be home.

Qualis artifex pereo

> Trans: "What an artist the world is losing with me!"
>
> cited by Suctonius, *The Twelve Caesars*, Nero 49; Loeb ed., 2:177

Michael had jet black hair and sorrowful brown eyes that sparkled when he smiled, which was often. Sprawled on his lounge chair every Saturday, he soaked up the sun while neighborhood girls lingered, serving iced tea and lemonade. Life seemed simply marvelous.

He was not stunning, but he was good-looking in a disheveled, youthful, rebellious sort of way. Teenagers gathered around him, sitting on the grass, playing badminton, or gleefully tossing Frisbees back and forth in the backyard. Most of all, they listened amorously to his stories of adventurous treks in Asia or climbing steep rock walls in Yosemite. Late that spring, just two weeks before the start of summer vacation, he graduated at the top of his class from one of the best medical schools in the country.

I had known Michael since I was nine. We grew up together, although he was two years older than me. Our parents were friends, and like him, I became an Eagle Scout, president of my high school class, and wore a leather-handled Ka-bar US Marine Corps knife on my shin when I went camping. I applied to medical school and stayed local, so I hung around him as much as possible. He introduced me to ancient Greek philosophy and French theater, and tutored me in computer sciences. I did more than look up to him; I worshipped him because he was good at everything. He even played harmonica and lead guitar to my piano, vocalizing harmonies that outmatched my wretched voice singing the blues in coffee shops.

Once, we were sitting in the living room of his apartment overlooking the park in our well-to-do Southern California neighborhood. We were just a few blocks from his parents' home. Souvenirs from his travels were scattered among ornately framed contemporary lithographs and a collection of books stacked on wooden shelves. I remember Jamie Cullum's soft jazz playing in the background.

I set my third bottle of beer on the coffee table.

"So," I said. "Graduation is coming up. What's going to be your specialty?"

"Psychiatry." He spoke as if there were no alternatives, as if no other specialties existed.

"Sounds boring," I said.

He rattled the ice in his Scotch before answering. "I have questions I need answers to."

"Psychiatry, jeez," I said. "You're working through endless analysis, rehashing ad-infinitum the old Jung versus Freud and Lacan stuff or— "

"You have it all wrong." Michael interrupted.

"Or," I insisted on finishing my sentence, "using mind-altering drugs to interfere with neurochemical pathways most people know nothing about."

A silence lingered. Michael knew I wanted to become a surgeon and that anything but instant gratification was foreign to me. He lowered his eyes. He was always quiet when he pondered his way to a convincing argument.

"Mind and body work together," he said softly, "but while the surgical repair of an artery or the artful removal of a gallbladder requires technical skill, good judgment, and able decision making, it can't compare to the personal creativity needed to doctor the perplexing and contradictory environments of the human psyche."

"What do you mean?" I said.

Michael set his glass on the table. "I mean that when people consult a psychiatrist, they are not only asking to feel good or to be healed, they are asking to fit into society."

"Huh?"

"They want to know where they stand regarding norms on society's emotional and behavioral bell curves. They don't say so directly, but they want to know if it's okay for them to be the way they are, or if they need to change...to reconsider their life history."

He paused as I weighed his words. I gazed past the open balcony door to examine the Mexican-tiled rooftops of his parents' hacienda home less than a block away. I stood to feel a warm breeze floating up through the eucalyptus trees.

"Of course, there is pathology," he continued. "DSM-classified mental illness, I mean. But I'm not talking about that. I mean that everyone carries pathological traits within them just waiting to be released. Most of the time, people ignore them. They become delusional about their own existence. Other times, those traits become manifest. Observers don't realize it unless behaviors are grossly outside the norm. What I am saying is that in all sense, most of us seem normal."

Thinking back, I can't help but conclude he was telling me something. He was reaching out in some odd *let me guide others so that I could guide myself* way. I should have probed his feelings. Instead, I challenged him.

"So, Michael, you're saying that everyone's living a lie."

"It's Hollywood," he retorted.

"That's hard to believe," I said. "I mean, it seems to me most people are happy. They go to work, school, and take vacations. There are couples everywhere." I walked to the bookshelf and picked up a black Akuaba fertility doll he had found in Ghana during one of his trips. Carved from ebony wood, its flat, oval head and annulated neck were attached to a short, rectangular body. "People get married," I said. "They have kids. They raise families. In the end, they retire to a golf community."

I presumed he would laugh at my pragmatism, but his face turned somber.

"It's all a lie," he said. He averted my gaze to look past me, outwards beyond the balcony. After another silence, he rose from the couch. There were fresh coffee stains on the armrest where he had been sitting. He placed his hands on his hips and arched his back to stretch.

"Where is it, though?" he said. "Where is the lie?"

His questions sounded rhetorical. He walked past me to shut the balcony door, then turned. He passed his hands through his hair and clasped them behind his neck. His elbows pointed forward when he faced me. I was surprised to hear him raise his voice.

"Is it a lie if my life is governed by a false self, even if I don't realize the false self is in command?" he said. "Is it wrong for me to become true to my Buddha nature, even if I'm not certain what that is?"

"Jeez, Michael, you ask yourself too many questions. Everything comes to you too easily. You enjoy life. Why ask questions to which there are no answers?"

Michael put his hands in his pockets and leaned his body into the corner of the room. "Well, my friend, if you had a choice – if you could have chosen your mother and father, would you have changed anything?"

I was the first person Michael's parents called on Monday, that third week in May. After his graduation celebrations, Michael went to his parents' house and hanged himself from a wooden beam in their living room. When I rushed through their door, I saw his body dangling lifelessly from the ceiling, casting alternating shadows of different intensities on the marble floor; shadows that changed with the position of the Pacific sunset fluttering on the horizon.

Moroccan Blue

"I love the taste of semen," Brigitte says, pouting her lips as only a French girl can. "Does that intimidate you?"

"I don't know," I say. "Should it?"

"It's not something guys like to hear." She stirs three teaspoons of sugar into an espresso. "I was with my boyfriend for seven years, but he dated other nurses. What about you?"

"I'm not married, if that's what you mean."

Brigitte sits forward, crossing her forearms on the table. There's that pout again.

"So, they assigned you to a singles resort," she says. "Sandy bays with blue-green waters at the foot of the Rif mountains. It's not a bad way to spend the summer."

"Well, it's my first real job since graduation, and the recruiters said Morocco was ideal for romance."

She cups her hands under her chin. I love the way she lifts her eyebrows when she smiles. Her blue eyes are blue like the azure sail of a Portuguese-man-of-war.

"I'm all ears," she purrs.
"Your eyes are stunning."
"I'm listening."
"Seriously, they're beautiful."

It's a Bogart-Bacall moment—seconds pass with no response.

"I like a man who is sincere—not very original, but sincere." Her sun-bleached hair bounces over her shoulders as she breaks out laughing. She brushes the curls back and furrows her brow. When she takes my hand, her smile vanishes into the parentheses at the corner of her mouth, but there is a playfulness in her voice. "So, tell me, doctor. Do you seriously think we can be an item?"

Her eyes glisten. Small beads of sweat gather on her temples. Even in the shade of the resort's First Aid office, the afternoon heat is smothering.

"It's a club for singles," she says, stroking my palm. "I don't think you're here to ogle me monogamously."

A hoard of shouting children burst in. "Come quick, there's been an accident!"

I jerk back my hand. "What?"

"A man is drowning."

Brigitte bolts from her chair and grabs the red and white emergency medical kit. She strains to carry it. The kids push and pull her toward the door. "Hurry," they shout.

"Hurry," she says, throwing me a look over her shoulder.

I grab an oxygen tank from the storage rack. The heavy steel cylinder is about two feet long and five inches in diameter. Lifting it onto my shoulder, I remember to shove the regulator into my back pocket and rush down the steps toward the beach. The tank weighs on my clavicle. I run past several couples lounging on their hammocks. Music plays from the adjoining bar. People move aside to let me through to the boardwalk.

About fifty feet in front of me, Brigitte stumbles. She picks herself up, and still gripping the toolbox, starts running again. "Hurry," the children scream. A younger one is crying.

Without flip-flops, my feet sink into the burning sand. I pant and plod across the open beach to catch up with my nurse. Sweat streams from her neck to the small of her back, shining like a thousand mirrors on her golden tan. She drags herself forward, kicking grit from thousands of crushed seashells in every direction.

An older child grabs the medical kit from her struggling hands and hoists it onto his shoulders.

"I couldn't carry it anymore," she gasps.

"It's okay," I say, catching my breath.

Several men are crouched by a teenager's body. Their chatter roars over the whoosh of the surf.

"We just pulled the boy out of the water," an older man says. Another takes the oxygen cylinder from my shoulder and drops it on the sand.

The kid looks like he's sleeping. He's maybe seventeen, with wavy black hair and stubble. The waves lick his ankles, and his legs are partially covered with wet gray slop. I grab him under the armpits and strain to pull him further onto shore.

"Move away!" I yell at the crowd. "Give me some room."

I deliver a precordial thump to the kid's chest. Holding my fist about ten inches off his breastbone, I deliver a second blow, but there is no response. I drop to my knees and begin chest compressions. And one, and two, and three, and four, and five, I count silently. Brigitte stands helplessly at the boy's feet.

I pause for a breath between compressions. "Have you ever given mouth-to-mouth?"

"No," she says. "Never."

"Take over then."

She kneels and stacks her palms on the kid's chest.

"Don't bend your elbows," I remind her. "Lean onto your arms."

"But, I've never done this before," she pleads.

"Give him five compressions, then pause," I say.

She pushes on the kid's chest and counts, "And one, and two, and three, and four, and five..."

"Okay, stop for a second." I pull a strand of seaweed from around the boy's neck and throw it aside. I tilt his head using a chin lift. With one hand on his forehead, I pinch his nostrils and take a deep breath before wrapping my lips around his mouth.

He retches as I exhale. It's more of a spasm than a retch, but he vomits all the same, and I cough violently, spitting and almost retching myself. I wipe my face with the back of my hand. Brigitte stops the chest compressions.

"Don't stop," I shout. "Keep going!"

The crowd circles. No one offers help, or if so, I don't notice.

I ignore the sand glued to my face and fight a dry heave as I wipe foul-smelling sticky goo from my nose. I dig in my knees and sit on my heels. The kid's eyes are open, but he doesn't move.

I put my mouth to his and exhale into what feels like a bottomless container. I can't feel his chest rise, so I try again.

Brigitte stops compressions and inches away from the boy. She's sobbing. I thump once more on the young man's chest.

"Brigitte, kneel across from me and try again," I give the kid another breath.

Nothing.

Brigitte crouches in the sand. She keeps tossing her shoulder straps back on to keep her breasts from popping out of her bathing suit. With the sun in her face, she looks at me through squinted eyes. Her cheeks are flushed and wet.

"And one, and two, and three..." She leans into the boy's chest. "Oh God," she cries.

"What's wrong?" I ask.

"I felt his ribs crack."

This is a disaster, I think. Fuck.

"He's not going to make it," I say to no one in particular. Brigitte stops counting.

"He's dead." A man from the crowd steps forward. "He's dead, I tell you."

"Maybe not," another answers. "They should continue."

"No," the first man urges, "he's dead, I say. He should not have been in the water anyway. He couldn't swim. Besides, only a fool goes in the water with an inner tube." He shakes his head in despair.

I stop my efforts and look up at the crowd. I'm still on my knees, holding back the tears. "I couldn't save him."

Brigitte shudders.

"You did your best," someone says.

"How do we know you're a doctor?" a woman asks.

I glare at her but I don't respond.

The police arrive, and onlookers describe what happened. Confusion reigns among shouts, arguments, and tears. "You should go back to the club," an officer says. I shoulder the oxygen bottle, and silently, Brigitte and I drag the unopened medical kit back to the First Aid office.

"He had blue eyes," she says when we arrive.

I close the door. Our lovemaking is immediately fierce and untamed, as if we could extinguish our anguish in the orgasmic bliss of a brief romance. We sleep that night in each other's arms, but in the morning, with tears running down her sunburned cheeks, she tells me she is leaving.

"Back to my boyfriend," she says. "I'm going home."

§

Permissions Acknowledgments

These stories first appeared in the following:

A Cold Little Secret – POTATO SOUP JOURNAL (February 2020)

A Death in Quito – ACTIVE MUSE (Pushcart Prize nominee, January 2020)

A Girl Named Ahh – RED FEZ 135 (May 2020)

Alone – CAFELIT (April 30, 2020)

Breakfast in Tokyo – FLASH FICTION MAGAZINE (January 25, 2021)

Does Anyone Sing at Easter – ACTIVE MUSE (January 2022).

Eve's Night Out – STRANDS (May 25 2020)

Forever Always – FICTION ON THE WEB (October 2021)

LIFE & DEATH: 30 STORIES ABOUT

Gingerbread Love – HOLIDAY DIGEST (December 5 2019)

Going South – COMMUTERLIT.COM (March 2020)

In Aristotle's footsteps – HEKTOEN INTERNATIONAL (January 31 2022)

Jungbu's Mother – FICTION ON THE WEB (December 18 2020)

Kansas City Ganges - FICTION on the WEB (September 2019

Kate Can't Fly – FEWER THAN 500 (January 2020)

Moroccan Blue –SCARLET LEAF REVIEW (February 2020)

My Guardian Angel – ACTIVE MUSE (March 2021)

My Sixtieth birthday – THE CABINET OF HEED (July 2020 Issue 37)

Never a Coward – ROCK AND ICE (November 2019)

Qualis artifex pereo – HEKTOEN INTERNATIONAL (March 2022)

Sarah's lesson: — HEKTOEN INTERNATIONAL (October 8 2020)

Serengeti 101 – CAFELIT (March 2022)

Six Months and Counting – DOWN IN THE DIRT (June 2022)

Something About Chanel – CAFELITMAGAZINE (January 19 2022)

Sticky Lips and the Stray Cat – CAFELITMAGAZINE (November 27 2021)

Tango – ADELAIDE LITERARY MAGAZINE (April 2020 Issue #35)

The Colonel's daughter – DOWN IN THE DIRT (April 1 2021)

The Deer Trail – HEKTOEN INTERNATIONAL (Fall 2020)

Too Late for a Kiss – FEWER THAN 500 (November 2019)

Unanswered Questions – DOWN IN THE DIRT (November 2020 Issue Pipe Dreams)

Whisper Red - FLASH FICTION MAGAZINE (November 2019)

§

Made in the USA
Monee, IL
02 November 2024